PLATE I.
The bud opened into a full-blown flower,
in the middle of which lay a beautiful child

The LITTLE MERMAID

AND·OTHER·FAIRY·TALES

Hans Christian Andersen

Illustrated by
W. HEATH ROBINSON

BARNES & NOBLE
NEW YORK

This 2016 edition printed for Barnes & Noble by
Sterling Publishing Co., Inc.

ISBN 978-1-4351-6368-3

Barnes & Noble, Inc.
122 Fifth Avenue
New York, NY 10011

Manufactured in China

3 5 7 9 10 8 6 4

www.sterlingpublishing.com

Cover and endpaper art by Kelly Thorn

Contents

LIST OF PLATES

List of Illustrations

THE LITTLE MERMAID

The Little Mermaid

AR OUT IN THE WIDE SEA,—WHERE THE WATER IS BLUE AS the loveliest cornflower, and clear as the purest crystal, where it is so deep that very, very many church-towers must be heaped one upon another in order to reach from the lowest depth to the surface above,—dwell the Mer-people.

Now you must not imagine that there is nothing but sand below the water: no, indeed, far from it! Trees and plants of wondrous beauty grow there, whose stems and leaves are so light, that they are waved to and fro by the slightest motion of the water, almost as if they were living beings. Fishes, great and small, glide in and out among the branches, just as birds fly about among our trees.

Where the water is deepest stands the palace of the Mer-King. The walls of this palace are of coral, and the high, pointed windows are of amber; the roof, however, is composed of mussel-shells, which, as the billows pass over them, are continually opening and shutting. This looks exceedingly pretty, especially as each of these mussel-shells contains a number of bright, glittering pearls, one only of which would be the most costly ornament in the diadem of a king in the upper world.

The Mer-King, who lived in this palace, had been for many years a widower; his old mother managed the household affairs for him. She was, on the whole, a sensible sort of a lady, although extremely proud of her high birth and station, on which account she wore twelve oysters on her tail, whilst the other inhabitants of the sea, even those of distinction, were allowed only six. In every other respect she merited unlimited praise, especially for the affection she showed to the six little princesses, her grand-daughters. These were all very beautiful children; the youngest was, however, the most lovely; her skin was as soft and delicate as a rose-leaf, her eyes were of as deep a blue as the sea, but like all other mermaids, she had no feet, her body ended in a tail like that of a fish.

She was on the whole a sensible sort of lady

The whole day long the children used to play in the spacious apartments of the palace, where beautiful flowers grew out of the walls on all sides around them. When the great amber windows were opened, fishes would swim into these apartments as swallows fly into our rooms; but the fishes were bolder than the swallows, they swam straight up to the little princesses, ate from their hands, and allowed themselves to be caressed.

In front of the palace there was a large garden, full of fiery red and dark blue trees, whose fruit glittered like gold, and whose flowers resembled a bright, burning sun. The sand that formed the soil of the garden was of a bright blue color, something like flames of sulfur; and a strangely beautiful blue was spread over the whole, so that one might have fancied oneself raised very high in the air, with the sky at once above and below, certainly not at the bottom of the sea. When the waters were quite still, the sun might be seen looking like a purple flower, out of whose cup streamed forth the light of the world.

Ate from their hands

Each of the little princesses had her own plot in the garden, where she might plant and sow at her pleasure. One chose hers to be made in the shape of a whale, another preferred the figure of a mermaid, but the youngest had hers quite round like the sun, and planted in it only those flowers that were red, as the sun seemed to her. She was certainly a singular child, very quiet and thoughtful. Whilst her sisters were adorning themselves with all sorts of gay things that came out of a ship which had been wrecked, she asked for nothing but a beautiful white marble statue of a boy, which had been found in it. She put the statue in her garden, and planted a red weeping willow by its side. The tree grew up quickly, and let its long boughs fall upon the bright blue ground, where ever-moving shadows played in violet hues, as if boughs and root were embracing.

Nothing pleased the little princess more than to hear about the world of human beings living above the sea. She made her

PLATE 2.
She put the statue in her garden

old grandmother tell her everything she knew about ships, towns, men, and land animals, and was particularly pleased when she heard that the flowers of the upper world had a pleasant fragrance (for the flowers of the sea are scentless), and that the woods were green, and the fishes fluttering among the branches of various gay colors, and that they could sing with a loud clear voice. The old lady meant birds, but she called them fishes, because her grandchildren, having never seen a bird, would not otherwise have understood her.

"When you have attained your fifteenth year," added she, "you will be permitted to rise to the surface of the sea; you will then sit by moonlight in the clefts of the rocks, see the ships sail by, and learn to distinguish towns and men."

The next year the eldest of the sisters reached this happy age, but the others—alas! the second sister was a year younger than the eldest, the third a year younger than the second, and so on; the youngest had still five whole years to wait till that joyful time should come when she also might rise to the surface of the water and see what was going on in the upper world; however, the eldest promised to tell the others of everything she might see, when the first day of her being of age arrived; for the grandmother gave them but little information, and there was so much that they wished to hear.

But none of all the sisters longed so ardently for the day when she should be released from childish restraint as the youngest, she who had longest to wait, and was so quiet and thoughtful. Many a night she stood by the open window, looking up through the clear blue water, whilst the fishes were leaping and playing around her. She could see the sun and the moon; their light was pale, but they appeared larger than they do to those who live in the upper world. If a shadow passed over them, she knew it must be either a whale or a ship sailing by full of human beings, who indeed little thought that, far beneath them, a little mermaid was passionately stretching forth her white hands towards their ship's keel.

The day had now arrived when the eldest princess had attained her fifteenth year, and was therefore allowed to rise up to the surface of the sea.

When she returned she had a thousand things to relate. Her chief pleasure had been to sit upon a sandbank in the moonlight, looking at the large town which lay on the coast, where lights were beaming like stars, and where music was playing; she had heard the distant noise of men and carriages, she had seen the high church-towers, had listened to the ringing of the bells; and just because she could not go there she longed the more after all these things.

How attentively did her youngest sister listen to her words! And when she next stood at night-time by her open window, gazing upward through the blue waters, she thought so intensely of the great noisy city that she fancied she could hear the church-bells ringing.

Next year the second sister received permission to swim wherever she pleased. She rose to the surface of the sea, just when the sun was setting; and this sight so delighted her, that she declared it to be more beautiful than anything else she had seen above the waters.

"The whole sky seemed tinged with gold," said she, "and it is impossible for me to describe to you the beauty of the clouds. Now red, now violet, they glided over me; but still more swiftly flew over the water a flock of white swans, just where the sun was descending; I looked after them, but the sun disappeared, and the bright rosy light on the surface of the sea and on the edges of the clouds was gradually extinguished."

It was now time for the third sister to visit the upper world. She was the boldest of the six, and ventured up a river. On its shores she saw green hills covered with woods and vineyards, from among which arose houses and castles; she heard the birds singing, and the sun shone with so much power, that she was continually obliged to plunge below, in order to cool her burning face. In a little bay she met with a number of children, who were bathing and jumping about; she would have joined in their gambols, but the children fled back to land in great terror, and a little black animal barked at her in such a manner, that she herself was frightened at last, and swam back to the sea. She could not, however, forget the green woods, the verdant hills, and the pretty children, who, although they had no fins, were swimming about in the river so fearlessly.

The fourth sister was not so bold, she remained in the open sea, and said on her return home she thought nothing could be more beautiful. She had seen ships sailing by, so far off that they looked like sea-gulls, she had watched the merry dolphins gamboling in the water, and the enormous whales, sending up into the air a thousand sparkling fountains.

The year after, the fifth sister attained her fifteenth year. Her birthday happened at a different season to that of her sisters; it was winter, the sea was of a green color, and immense icebergs were floating on its surface. These, she said, looked like pearls; they were, however, much larger than the church-towers in the land of human beings. She sat down upon one of these pearls, and let the wind play with her long hair, but then all the ships hoisted their sails in terror, and escaped as quickly as possible. In the evening the sky was covered with sails; and whilst the great mountains of ice alternately sank and rose again, and beamed with a reddish glow, flashes of lightning burst forth from the clouds, and the thunder rolled on, peal after peal. The sails of all the ships were instantly furled, and horror and affright reigned on board, but the princess sat still on the iceberg, looking unconcernedly at the blue zig-zag of the flashes.

The first time that either of these sisters rose out of the sea, she was quite enchanted at the sight of so many new and beautiful objects, but the novelty was soon over, and it was not long ere their own home appeared more attractive than the upper world, for there only did they find everything agreeable.

Many an evening would the five sisters rise hand in hand from the depths of the ocean. Their voices were far sweeter than any human voice, and when a storm was coming on, they would swim in front of the ships, and sing,—oh! how sweetly did they sing! describing the happiness of those who lived at the bottom of the sea, and entreating the sailors not to be afraid, but to come down to them.

The mariners, however, did not understand their words; they fancied the song was only the whistling of the wind, and thus they lost the hidden glories of the sea; for if their ships were wrecked, all on board were drowned, and none but dead men ever entered the Mer-King's palace.

Whilst the sisters were swimming at evening-time, the youngest would remain motionless and alone, in her father's palace, looking up after them. She would have wept, but mermaids cannot weep, and therefore, when they are troubled, suffer infinitely more than human beings do.

"Oh, if I were but fifteen!" sighed she, "I know that I should love the upper world and its inhabitants so much."

At last the time she had so longed for arrived.

"Well, now it is your turn," said the grandmother; "come here, that I may adorn you like your sisters." And she wound around her hair a wreath of white lilies, whose every petal was the half of a pearl, and then commanded eight large oysters to fasten themselves to the princess's tail, in token of her high rank.

"But that is so very uncomfortable!" said the little princess.

"One must not mind slight inconveniences when one wishes to look well," said the old lady.

How willingly would the princess have given up all this splendor, and exchanged her heavy crown for the red flowers of her garden, which were so much more becoming to her. But she dared not do so. "Farewell," said she; and she rose from the sea, light as a flake of foam.

When, for the first time in her life, she appeared on the surface of the water, the sun had just sunk below the horizon, the clouds were beaming with bright golden and rosy hues, the evening star was shining in the pale western sky, the air was mild and refreshing, and the sea as smooth as a looking-glass. A large ship with three masts lay on the still waters; one sail only was unfurled, but not a breath was stirring, and the sailors were quietly seated on the cordage and ladders of the vessel. Music and song resounded from the deck, and after it grew dark hundreds of lamps all on a sudden burst forth into light, whilst innumerable flags were fluttering overhead. The little mermaid swam close up to the captain's cabin, and every now and then when the ship was raised by the motion of the water, she could look through the clear window panes. She saw within many richly dressed men; the handsomest among them was a young prince with large black eyes. He could not certainly be more than sixteen years old, and it was in honor of his birthday that a grand festival was being celebrated. The crew were dancing on the deck, and when the young prince appeared among them, a hundred rockets were sent up into the air, turning night into day, and so terrifying the little mermaid, that for some minutes she plunged beneath the water. However, she soon raised her little head again, and then it seemed as if all the stars were falling down upon her. Such a fiery shower she had never even seen before, never had she heard that men possessed such wonderful powers. Large suns revolved around her, bright fishes swam in the air, and everything was reflected perfectly on the clear surface of the sea. It was so light in the ship, that everything could be seen distinctly. Oh, how happy the young prince was! He shook hands with the sailors, laughed and jested with them, whilst sweet notes of music mingled with the silence of night.

It was now late, but the little mermaid could not tear herself away from the ship and the handsome young prince. She remained looking through the cabin window, rocked to and fro by the waves. There was a foaming and fermentation in the depths beneath, and the ship began to move on faster; the sails were spread, the waves rose high, thick clouds gathered over the sky, and the noise of distant thunder was heard. The sailors perceived that a storm was coming on, so they again furled the sails. The great vessel was tossed about on the tempestuous ocean like a light boat, and the waves rose to an immense height, towering over the ship, which alternately sank beneath and rose above them. To the little mermaid this seemed most delightful, but the ship's crew thought very differently. The vessel cracked, the stout masts bent under the violence of the billows, the waters rushed in. For a minute the ship tottered to and fro, then the main-mast broke, as if it had been a reed; the ship turned over, and was filled with water. The little mermaid now perceived that the crew was in danger, for she herself was forced to beware of the beams and splinters torn from the vessel, and floating about on the waves. But at the same time it became pitch dark so that she could not distinguish anything; presently, however, a dreadful flash of lightning disclosed to her the whole of the wreck. Her eyes sought the young prince—the same instant the ship sank to the bottom. At first she was delighted, thinking that the prince must now come to her abode; but she soon remembered that man cannot live in water, and that therefore if the prince ever entered her palace, it would be as a corpse.

"Die! no, he must not die!" She swam through the fragments with which the water was strewn regardless of the danger she was incurring, and at last found the prince all but exhausted, and with great difficulty keeping his head above water. He had already closed his eyes, and must inevitably have been drowned, had not the little mermaid come to his rescue. She seized hold of him and kept him above water, suffering the current to bear them on together.

Towards morning the storm was hushed; no trace, however, remained of the ship. The sun rose like fire out of the sea; his beams seemed to restore color to the prince's cheeks, but his eyes were still closed. The mermaid kissed his high forehead and stroked his wet hair away from his face. He looked like the marble statue in her garden; she kissed him again and wished most fervently that he might recover.

She now saw the dry land with its mountains glittering with snow. A green wood extended along the coast, and at the entrance of the wood stood a chapel or convent, she could not be sure which. Citron and lemon trees grew in the garden adjoining it, an avenue of tall palm trees led up to the door. The sea here formed a little bay, in which the water was quite smooth but very deep, and under the cliffs there were dry, firm sands. Hither swam the little mermaid with the seemingly dead prince; she laid him upon the warm sand, and took care to place his head high, and to turn his face to the sun.

The bells began to ring in the large white building which stood before her, and a number of young girls came out to walk in the garden. The mermaid went away from the shore, hid herself behind some stones, covered her head with foam, so that her little face could not be seen, and watched the prince with unremitting attention.

It was not long before one of the young girls approached. She seemed quite frightened at finding the prince in this state, apparently dead; soon, however, she recovered herself, and ran back to call her sisters. The little mermaid saw that the prince revived, and that all around smiled kindly and joyfully upon him—for her, however, he looked not, he knew not that it was she who had saved him, and when the prince was taken into the house she felt so sad, that she immediately plunged beneath the water, and returned to her father's palace.

If she had been before quiet and thoughtful, she now grew still more so. Her sisters asked her what she had seen in the upper world, but she made no answer.

Many an evening she rose to the place where she had left the prince. She saw the snow on the mountains melt, the fruits in the garden ripen and gathered, but the prince she never saw, so she always returned sorrowfully to her subterranean abode. Her only pleasure was to sit in her little garden gazing on the beautiful statue so like the prince. She cared no longer for her flowers; they grew up in wild luxuriance, covered the steps, and entwined their long stems and tendrils among the boughs of the trees, so that her whole garden became a bower.

At last, being unable to conceal her sorrow any longer, she revealed the secret to one of her sisters, who told it to the other princesses, and they to some of their friends. Among them was a young mermaid who recollected the prince, having been an eye-witness herself to the festivities in the ship; she knew also in what country the prince lived, and the name of its king.

Many an evening she rose
to the place

"Come, little sister!" said the princesses, and embracing her, they rose together arm in arm, out of the water, just in front of the prince's palace.

This palace was built of bright yellow stones, a flight of white marble steps led from it down to the sea. A gilded cupola crowned the building, and white marble figures, which might almost have been taken for real men and women, were placed among the pillars surrounding it. Through the clear glass of the high windows one might look into magnificent apartments hung with silken curtains, the walls adorned with magnificent paintings. It was a real treat to the little royal mermaids to behold so splendid an abode; they gazed through the windows of one of the largest rooms, and in the center saw a fountain playing, whose waters sprang up so high as to reach the glittering cupola above, through which the sunbeams fell dancing on the water, and brightening the pretty plants which grew around it.

The little mermaid now knew where her beloved prince dwelt, and henceforth she went there almost every evening. She often approached nearer the land than her sisters had ventured, and even swam up the narrow channel that flowed under the marble balcony. Here on a bright moonlight night, she would watch the young prince, who believed himself alone.

Sometimes she saw him sailing on the water in a gaily painted boat with many colored flags waving above. She would then hide among the green reeds which grew on the banks, listening to his voice, and if any one in the boat noticed the rustling of her long silver veil, which was caught now and then by the light breeze, they only fancied it was a swan flapping his wings.

Many a night when the fishermen were casting their nets by the beacon's light, she heard them talking of the prince, and relating the noble actions he had performed. She was then so happy, thinking how she had saved his life when struggling with the waves, and remembering how his head had rested on her bosom, and how she had kissed him when he knew nothing of it, and could never even dream of such a thing.

Human beings became more and more dear to her every day; she wished that she were one of them. Their world seemed to her much larger than that of the mer-people; they could fly over the ocean in their ships, as well as climb to the summits of those high mountains that rose above the clouds; and their wooded domains extended much farther than a mermaid's eye could penetrate.

There were many things that she wished to hear explained, but her sisters could not give her any satisfactory answer; she was again obliged to have recourse to the old queen-mother, who knew a great deal about the upper world, which she used to call "the country above the sea."

"Do men when they are not drowned live for ever?" she asked one day. "Do they not die as we do, who live at the bottom of the sea?"

"Yes," was the grandmother's reply, "they must die like us, and their life is much shorter than ours. We live to the age of three hundred years, but when we die, we become foam on the sea, and are not allowed even to share a grave among those that are dear to us. We have no immortal souls, we can never live again, and are like the grass which, when once cut down, is withered for ever. Human beings, on the contrary, have souls that continue to live when their bodies become dust, and as we rise out of the water to admire the abode of man, they ascend to glorious unknown dwellings in the skies which we are not permitted to see."

"Why have not *we* immortal souls?" asked the little mermaid. "I would willingly give up my three hundred years to be a human being for only one day, thus to become entitled to that heavenly world above."

"You must not think of that," answered her grandmother, "it is much better as it is; we live longer and are far happier than human beings."

"So I must die, and be dashed like foam over the sea, never to rise again and hear the gentle murmur of the ocean, never again see the beautiful flowers and the bright sun! Tell me, dear grandmother, are there no means by which I may obtain an immortal soul?"

"No!" replied the old lady. "It is true that if thou couldst so win the affections of a human being as to become dearer to him than either father or mother; if he loved thee with all his heart, and promised whilst the priest joined his hands with thine to be always faithful to thee; then his soul would flow into thine, and thou wouldst then become partaker of human bliss. But that can never be! for what in our eyes is the most beautiful part of our body, the tail, the inhabitants of the earth think hideous, they cannot bear it. To appear handsome to them, the body must have two clumsy props which they call legs."

The little mermaid sighed and looked mournfully at the scaly part of her form, otherwise so fair and delicate.

"We are happy," added the old lady, "we shall jump and swim about merrily for three hundred years; that is a long time, and afterwards we shall repose peacefully in death. This evening we have a court ball."

The ball which the queen-mother spoke of was far more splendid than any that earth has ever seen. The walls of the saloon were of crystal, very thick, but yet very clear; hundreds of large mussel-shells were planted in rows along them; these shells were some of rose-color, some green as grass, but all sending forth a bright light, which not only illuminated the whole apartment, but also shone through the glassy walls so as to light up the waters around for a great space, and making the scales of the numberless fishes, great and small, crimson and purple, silver and gold-colored, appear more brilliant than ever.

Through the center of the saloon flowed a bright, clear stream, on the surface of which danced mermen and mermaids to the melody of their own sweet voices, voices far sweeter than those of the dwellers upon earth. The little princess sang more harmoniously than any other, and they clapped their hands and applauded her. She was pleased at this, for she knew well that there was neither on earth or in the sea a more beautiful voice than hers. But her thoughts soon returned to the world above her: she could not forget the handsome prince; she could not control her sorrow at not having an immortal soul. She stole away from her father's palace, and whilst all was joy within, she sat alone lost in thought in her little neglected garden. On a sudden she heard the tones of horns resounding over the water far away in the distance, and she said to herself, "Now he is going out to hunt, he whom I love more than my father and my mother, with whom my thoughts are constantly occupied, and to whom I would so willingly trust the happiness of my life! All! all, will I risk to win him—and an immortal soul! Whilst my sisters are still dancing in the palace, I will go to the enchantress whom I have hitherto feared so much, but who is, nevertheless, the only person who can advise and help me."

So the little mermaid left the garden, and went to the foaming whirlpool beyond which dwelt the enchantress. She had never been this way before—neither flowers nor sea-grass bloomed along her path; she had to traverse an extent of bare grey sand till she reached the whirlpool, whose waters were eddying and whizzing like mill-wheels, tearing everything they could seize along with them into the abyss below. She was obliged to make her way through this horrible place, in order to arrive at the territory of the enchantress. Then she had to pass through a boiling, slimy bog, which the enchantress called her turf-moor: her house stood in a wood beyond this, and a strange abode it was. All the trees and bushes around were polypi, looking like hundred-headed serpents shooting up out of the ground; their branches were long slimy arms with fingers of worms, every member, from the root to the uttermost tip, ceaselessly moving and extending on all sides. Whatever they seized they fastened upon so that it could not loosen itself from their grasp. The little mermaid stood still for a minute looking at this horrible wood; her heart beat with fear, and she would certainly have returned without attaining her object, had she not remembered the prince—and immortality. The thought gave her new courage, she bound up her long waving hair, that the polypi might not catch hold of it, crossed her delicate arms over her bosom, and, swifter than a fish can glide through the water, she passed these unseemly trees, who stretched their eager arms after her in vain. She could not, however, help seeing that every polypus had something in his grasp, held as firmly by a thousand little arms as if enclosed by iron bands. The whitened skeletons of a number of human beings who had been drowned in the sea, and had sunk into the abyss, grinned horribly from the arms of these polypi; helms, chests, skeletons of land animals were also held in their embrace; among other things might be seen even a little mermaid whom they had seized and strangled! What a fearful sight for the unfortunate princess!

But she got safely through this wood of horrors, and then arrived at a slimy place, where immense, fat snails were crawling about, and in the midst of this place stood a house built of the bones of unfortunate people who had been shipwrecked. Here sat the witch caressing a toad in the same manner as some persons would a pet bird. The ugly fat snails she called her chickens, and she permitted them to crawl about her.

"I know well what you would ask of me," said she to the little princess. "Your wish is foolish enough, yet it shall be fulfilled, though its accomplishment is sure to bring misfortune on you, my fairest princess. You wish to get rid of your tail, and to have instead two stilts like those of human beings, in order that a young prince may fall in love with you, and that you may obtain an immortal soul. Is it not so?" Whilst the witch spoke these words, she laughed so violently that her pet toad and snails fell from her lap. "You come just at the right time," continued she; "had you come after sunset, it would not have been in my power to have helped you before another year. I will prepare for you a drink with which you must swim to land, you must sit down upon the shore and swallow it, and then your tail will fall and shrink up to the things which men call legs. This transformation will, however, be very painful; you will feel as though a sharp knife passed through your body. All who look on you after you have been thus changed will say that you are the loveliest child of earth they have ever seen; you will retain your peculiar undulating movements, and no dancer will move so lightly, but every step you take will cause you pain all but unbearable; it will seem to you as though you were walking on the sharp edges of swords, and your blood will flow. Can you endure all this suffering? If so, I will grant your request."

"Yes, I will," answered the princess, with a faltering voice; for she remembered her dear prince, and the immortal soul which her suffering might win.

"Only consider," said the witch, "that you can never again become a mermaid, when once you have received a human form. You may never return to your sisters, and your father's palace; and unless you shall win the prince's love to such a degree that he shall leave father and mother for you, that you shall be mixed up with all his thoughts and wishes, and unless the priest join your hands, so that you become man and wife, you will never obtain the immortality you seek. The morrow of the day on which he is united to another will see your death; your heart will break with sorrow, and you will be changed to foam on the sea."

"Still I will venture!" said the little mermaid, pale and trembling as a dying person.

"Besides all this, I must be paid, and it is no slight thing that I require for my trouble. Thou hast the sweetest voice of all the dwellers in the sea, and thou thinkest by its means to charm the prince; this voice, however, I demand as my recompense. The best thing thou possessest I require in exchange for my magic drink; for I shall be obliged to sacrifice my own blood, in order to give it the sharpness of a two-edged sword."

"But if you take my voice from me," said the princess, "what have I left with which to charm the prince?"

"Thy graceful form," replied the witch, "thy modest gait, and speaking eyes. With such as these, it will be easy to infatuate a vain human heart. Well now! hast thou lost courage? Put out thy little tongue, that I may cut it off, and take it for myself, in return for my magic drink."

"Be it so!" said the princess, and the witch took up her caldron, in order to mix her potion. "Cleanliness is a good thing," remarked she, as she began to rub the caldron with a handful of toads and snails. She then scratched her bosom, and let the black blood trickle down into the caldron, every moment throwing in new ingredients, the smoke from the mixture assuming such horrible forms, as were enough to fill beholders with terror, and a moaning and groaning proceeding from it, which might be compared to the weeping of crocodiles. The magic drink at length became clear and transparent as pure water; it was ready.

"Here it is!" said the witch to the princess, cutting out her tongue at the same moment. The poor little mermaid was now dumb: she could neither sing nor speak.

If the polypi should attempt to seize you, as you pass through my little grove," said the witch, "you have only to sprinkle some of this magic drink over them, and their arms will burst into a thousand pieces." But the princess had no need of this counsel, for the polypi drew hastily back, as soon as they perceived the bright phial, that glittered in her hand like a star; thus she passed safely through the formidable wood over the moor, and across the foaming mill-stream.

She now looked once again at her father's palace; the lamps in the saloon were extinguished, and all the family were asleep. She would not go in, for she could not speak if she did; she was about to leave her home for ever; her heart was ready to break with sorrow at the thought; she stole into the garden, plucked a flower from the bed of each of her sisters as a remembrance, kissed her hand again and again, and then rose through the dark blue waters to the world above.

The sun had not yet risen when she arrived at the prince's dwelling, and ascended those well-known marble steps. The moon still shone in the sky when the little mermaid drank off the wonderful liquid contained in her phial. She felt it run through her like a sharp knife, and she fell down in a swoon. When the sun rose, she awoke; and felt a burning pain in all her limbs, but—she saw standing close to her the object of her love, the handsome young prince, whose coal-black eyes were fixed inquiringly upon her. Full of shame she cast down her own, and perceived, instead of the long fish-like tail she had hitherto borne, two slender legs; but she was quite naked, and tried in vain to cover herself with her long thick hair. The prince asked who she was, and how she had got there; and she, in reply, smiled and gazed upon him with her bright blue eyes, for alas! she could not speak. He then led her by the hand into the palace. She found that the witch had told her true—she felt as though she were walking on the edges of sharp swords, but she bore the pain willingly; on she passed, light as a zephyr, and all who saw her wondered at her light, undulating movements.

When she entered the palace, rich clothes of muslin and silk were brought to her; she was lovelier than all who dwelt there,

When the sun arose, she awoke

but she could neither speak nor sing. Some female slaves, gaily dressed in silk and gold brocade, sang before the prince and his royal parents; and one of them distinguished herself by her clear sweet voice, which the prince applauded by clapping his hands. This made the little mermaid very sad, for she knew that she used to sing far better than the young slave. "Alas!" thought she, "if he did but know that, for his sake, I have given away my voice for ever."

The slaves began to dance; our lovely little mermaiden then arose, stretched out her delicate white arms, and hovered gracefully about the room. Every motion displayed more and more the perfect symmetry and elegance of her figure; and the expression which beamed in her speaking eyes touched the hearts of the spectators far more than the song of the slaves.

All present were enchanted, but especially the young prince, who called her his dear little foundling. And she danced again and again, although every step cost her excessive pain. The prince then said she should always be with him; and accordingly a sleeping-place was prepared for her on velvet cushions in the anteroom of his own apartment.

The prince caused a suit of male apparel to be made for her, in order that she might accompany him in his rides; so together they traversed the fragrant woods, where green boughs brushed against their shoulders, and the birds sang merrily among the fresh leaves. With him she climbed up steep mountains, and although her tender feet bled, so as to be remarked by the attendants, she only smiled, and followed her dear prince to the heights, whence they could see the clouds chasing each other beneath them, like a flock of birds migrating to other countries.

During the night she would, when all in the palace were at rest, walk down the marble steps, in order to cool her feet in the deep waters; she would then think of those beloved ones who dwelt in the lower world.

One night, as she was thus bathing her feet, her sisters swam together to the spot, arm in arm and singing, but alas! so mournfully! She beckoned to them, and they immediately recognized her, and told her how great was the mourning in her father's house for her loss. From this time the sisters visited her every night; and once they brought with them the old grandmother, who had not seen the upper world for a great many years; they likewise brought their father, the Mer-King, with his crown on his head; but these two old people did not venture near enough to land to be able to speak to her.

The little mermaiden became dearer and dearer to the prince every day; but he only looked upon her as a sweet, gentle child, and the thought of making her his wife never entered his head. And yet his wife she must be, ere she could receive an immortal soul; his wife she must be, or she would change into foam, and be driven restlessly over the billows of the sea!

"Dost thou not love me above all others?" her eyes seemed to ask, as he pressed her fondly in his arms, and kissed her lovely brow.

"Yes," the prince would say, "thou art dearer to me than any other, for no one is as good as thou art! Thou lovest me so much; and thou art so like a young maiden whom I have seen but once, and may never see again. I was on board a ship, which was wrecked by a sudden tempest; the waves threw me on the shore, near a holy temple, where a number of young girls are occupied constantly with religious services. The youngest of them found me on the shore, and saved my life. I saw her only once, but her image is vividly impressed upon my memory, and her alone can I love. But she belongs to the holy temple; and thou who resemblest her so much hast been given to me for consolation; never will we be parted!"

"Alas! he does not know that it was I who saved his life," thought the little mermaiden, sighing deeply; "I bore him over the wild waves, into the wooded bay, where the holy temple stood; I sat behind the rocks, waiting till some one should come. I saw the pretty maiden approach, whom he loves more than me,"—and again she heaved a deep sigh, for she could not weep. "He said that the young girl belongs to the holy temple; she never comes out into the world, so they cannot meet each other again,—and I am always with him, see him daily; I will love him, and devote my whole life to him."

"So the prince is going to be married to the beautiful daughter of the neighboring king," said the courtiers, "that is why he is having that splendid ship fitted out. It is announced that he wishes to travel, but in reality he goes to see the princess; a numerous retinue will accompany him." The little mermaiden smiled at these and similar conjectures, for she knew the prince's intentions better than any one else.

"I must go," he said to her, "I must see the beautiful princess; my parents require me to do so; but they will not compel me to marry her, and bring her home as my bride. And it is quite impossible for me to love her, for she cannot be so like the beautiful girl in the temple as thou art; and if I were obliged to choose, I should prefer thee, my little silent foundling, with the speaking eyes." And he kissed her rosy lips, played with her locks, and folded her in his arms, whereupon arose in her heart a sweet vision of human happiness, and immortal bliss.

"Thou art not afraid of the sea, art thou, my sweet silent child?" asked he tenderly, as they stood together in the splendid ship, which was to take them to the country of the neighboring king. And then he told her of the storms that sometimes agitate the waters; of the strange fishes that inhabit the deep, and of the wonderful things seen by divers. But she smiled at his words, for she knew better than any child of earth what went on in the depths of the ocean.

At night-time, when the moon shone brightly, and when all on board were fast asleep, she sat in the ship's gallery, looking down into the sea. It seemed to her, as she gazed through the foamy track made by the ship's keel, that she saw her father's palace, and her grandmother's silver crown. She then saw her sisters rise out of the water, looking sorrowful and stretching out their hands towards her. She nodded to them, smiled, and would have explained that everything was going on quite according to her wishes; but just then the cabin boy approached, upon which the sisters plunged beneath the water so suddenly that the boy thought what he had seen on the waves was nothing but foam.

The next morning the ship entered the harbor of the king's splendid capital. Bells were rung, trumpets sounded, and soldiers marched in procession through the city, with waving banners, and glittering bayonets. Every day witnessed some new entertainments, balls and parties followed each other; the princess, however, was not yet in the town; she had been sent to a distant convent for education, and had there been taught the practice of all royal virtues. At last she arrived at the palace.

The little mermaid had been anxious to see this unparalleled princess; and she was now obliged to confess that she had never before seen so beautiful a creature.

The skin of the princess was so white and delicate that the veins might be seen through it, and her dark eyes sparkled beneath a pair of finely formed eye-brows.

"It is herself!" exclaimed the prince, when they met, "it is she who saved my life, when I lay like a corpse on the sea shore!" and he pressed his blushing bride to his beating heart.

"Oh, I am all too happy!" said he to his dumb foundling. "What I never dared to hope for has come to pass. Thou must rejoice in my happiness, for thou lovest me more than all others who surround me."—And the little mermaid kissed his hand in silent sorrow; it seemed to her as if her heart was breaking already, although the morrow of his marriage-day, which must inevitably see her death, had not yet dawned.

Again rung the church-bells, whilst heralds rode through the streets of the capital, to announce the approaching bridal. Odorous flames burned in silver candlesticks on all the altars; the priests swung their golden censers; and bride and bridegroom joined hands, whilst the holy words that united them were spoken. The little mermaid, clad in silk and cloth of gold, stood behind the princess, and held the train of the bridal dress; but her ear heard nothing of the solemn music; her eye saw not the holy ceremony; she remembered her approaching end, she remembered that she had lost both this world and the next.

That very same evening bride and bridegroom went on board the ship; cannons were fired, flags waved with the breeze, and in the center of the deck stood a magnificent pavilion of purple and cloth of gold, fitted up with the richest and softest couches. Here the princely pair were to spend the night. A favorable wind swelled the sails, and the ship glided lightly over the blue waters.

As soon as it was dark, colored lamps were hung out and dancing began on the deck. The little mermaid was thus involuntarily reminded of what she had seen the first time she rose to the upper world. The spectacle that now presented itself was equally splendid—and she was obliged to join in the dance, hovering lightly as a bird over the ship boards. All applauded her, for never had she danced with more enchanting grace. Her little feet suffered extremely, but she no longer felt the pain; the anguish her heart suffered was much greater. It was the last evening she might see him, for whose sake she had forsaken her home and all her family, had given away her beautiful voice, and suffered daily the most violent pain—all without his having the least suspicion of it. It was the last evening that she might breathe the same atmosphere in which he, the beloved one, lived; the last evening when she might behold the deep blue sea, and the starry heavens—an eternal night, in which she might neither think nor dream, awaited her. And all was joy in the ship; and she, her heart filled with thoughts of death and annihilation, smiled and danced with the others, till past midnight. Then the prince kissed his lovely bride, and arm in arm they entered the magnificent tent prepared for their repose.

All was now still; the steersman alone stood at the ship's helm. The little mermaid leaned her white arms on the gallery, and looked towards the east, watching for the dawn; she well knew that the first sunbeam would witness her dissolution. She saw her sisters rise out of the sea; deadly pale were their features;

and their long hair no more fluttered over their shoulders, it had all been cut off.

"We have given it to the witch," said they, "to induce her to help thee, so that thou mayest not die. She has given to us a penknife: here it is! Before the sun rises, thou must plunge it into the prince's heart; and when his warm blood trickles down upon thy feet they will again be changed to a fish-like tail; thou wilt once more become a mermaid, and wilt live thy full three hundred years, ere thou changest to foam on the sea. But hasten! either he or thou must die before sunrise. Our aged mother mourns for thee so much her grey hair has fallen off through sorrow, as ours fell before the scissors of the witch. Kill the prince, and come down to us! Hasten! hasten! dost thou not see the red streaks on the eastern sky, announcing the near approach of the sun? A few minutes more and he rises, and then all will be over with thee." At these words they sighed deeply and vanished.

The little mermaid drew aside the purple curtains of the pavilion, where lay the bride and bridegroom; bending over them, she kissed the prince's forehead, and then glancing at the sky, she saw that the dawning light became every moment brighter. The prince's lips unconsciously murmured the name of his bride— he was dreaming of her, and her only, whilst the fatal penknife trembled in the hand of the unhappy mermaid. All at once, she threw far out into the sea that instrument of death; the waves rose like bright blazing flames around, and the water where it fell seemed tinged with blood. With eyes fast becoming dim and fixed, she looked once more at her beloved prince; then plunged from the ship into the sea, and felt her body slowly but surely dissolving into foam.

The sun rose from his watery bed; his beams fell so softly and warmly upon her, that our little mermaid was scarcely sensible of dying. She still saw the glorious sun; and over her head hovered a thousand beautiful, transparent forms; she could still distinguish the white sails of the ship, and the bright red clouds in the sky; the voices of those airy creatures above her had a melody so sweet and soothing, that a human ear would be as little able to catch the sound as her eye was capable of distinguishing their forms; they hovered around her without wings, borne by their own lightness through the air. The little mermaid at last saw that she had a body as transparent as theirs; and felt herself raised gradually from the foam of the sea to higher regions.

"Where are they taking me?" asked she, and her words sounded just like the voices of those heavenly beings.

"Speak you to the daughters of air?" was the answer. "The mermaid has no immortal soul, and can only acquire that heavenly gift by winning the love of one of the sons of men; her immortality depends upon union with man. Neither do the daughters of air possess immortal souls, but they can acquire them by their own good deeds. We fly to hot countries, where the children of earth are sinking under sultry pestilential breezes— our fresh cooling breath revives them. We diffuse ourselves through the atmosphere; we perfume it with the delicious fragrance of flowers; and thus spread delight and health over the earth. By doing good in this manner for three hundred years, we win immortality, and receive a share of the eternal bliss of human beings. And thou, poor little mermaid! who, following the impulse of thine own heart, hast done and suffered so much, thou art now raised to the airy world of spirits, that

PLATE 3.
With the rest of the children of air,
soared high above the rosy cloud

by performing deeds of kindness for three hundred years, thou mayest acquire an immortal soul."

The little mermaid stretched out her transparent arms to the sun; and, for the first time in her life, tears moistened her eyes.

And now again all were awake and rejoicing in the ship; she saw the prince, with his pretty bride; they had missed her; they looked sorrowfully down on the foamy waters, as if they knew she had plunged into the sea; unseen she kissed the bridegroom's forehead, smiled upon him, and then, with the rest of the children of air, soared high above the rosy cloud which was sailing so peacefully over the ship.

"After three hundred years we shall fly in the kingdom of Heaven!"

"We may arrive there even sooner," whispered one of her sisters. "We fly invisibly through the dwellings of men, where there are children; and whenever we find a good child, who gives pleasure to his parents and deserves their love, the good God shortens our time of probation. No child is aware that we are flitting about his room, and that whenever joy draws from us a smile, a year is struck out of our three hundred. But when we see a rude naughty child, we weep bitter tears of sorrow, and every tear we shed adds a day to our time of probation."

The swallow soared high into the air

ONCE UPON A TIME THERE LIVED A YOUNG WIFE WHO LONGED exceedingly to possess a little child of her own, so she went to an old witch-woman and said to her, "I wish so very much to have a child, a little tiny child; won't you give me one, old mother?"

"Oh, with all my heart!" replied the witch. "Here is a barley-corn for you; it is not exactly of the same sort as those that grow on the farmer's fields, or that are given to the fowls in the poultry yard, but do you sow it in a flower-pot, and then you shall see what you shall see!"

"Thank you, thank you!" cried the woman, and she gave the witch a silver sixpence, and then having returned home sowed the barley-corn as she had been directed, whereupon a large and beautiful flower immediately shot forth from the flower-pot. It looked like a tulip, but the petals were tightly folded up; it was still in bud.

"What a lovely flower!" exclaimed the peasant-woman, and she kissed the pretty red and yellow leaves, and as she kissed them the flower gave a loud report and opened. It was indeed a tulip, but on the small green pointal in the center of the flower there sat a little tiny girl, so pretty and delicate, but her whole body scarcely bigger than the young peasant's thumb. So she called her Thumbelina.

A pretty varnished walnut-shell was given her as a cradle, blue violet leaves served as her mattresses, and a rose-leaf was her coverlet; here she slept at night, but in the daytime she played on the table. The peasant-wife had filled a plate with water, and laid flowers in it, their blossoms bordering the edge of the plate, while the stalks lay in the water; on the surface floated a large tulip-leaf, and on it Thumbelina might sit and sail from one side of the plate to the other, two white horse hairs having been given her for oars. That looked quite charming! And Thumbelina could sing too, and she sang in such low sweet tones as never were heard before.

One night, while she was lying in her pretty bed, a great ugly toad came hopping in through the broken window-pane. The toad was such a great creature, old and withered-looking, and wet too; she hopped at once down upon the table where Thumbelina lay sleeping under the red rose petal.

"That is just the wife for my son," said the toad; and she seized hold of the walnut-shell, with Thumbelina in it, and hopped away with her through the broken pane down into the garden. Here flowed a broad stream; its banks were muddy and swampy, and it was amongst this mud that the old toad and her son dwelt. Ugh, how hideous and deformed he was! just like his mother.

"Coax, coax, brekke-ke-kex!" was all he could find to say on seeing the pretty little maiden in the walnut-shell.

"Don't make such a riot, or you'll wake her!" said old mother toad. "She may easily run away from us, for she is as light as a swan-down feather. I'll tell you what we'll do; we'll take her out into the brook, and set her down on one of the large water-lily

"That is just the wife for my son," said the toad

leaves; it will be like an island to her, who is so light and small. Then she cannot run away from us, and we can go and get ready the state-rooms down under the mud, where you and she are to dwell together."

Out in the brook there grew many water-lilies, with their broad green leaves, each of which seemed to be floating over the water. The leaf which was the farthest from the shore was also the largest; to it swam old mother toad, and on it she set the walnut-shell, with Thumbelina.

The poor little tiny creature awoke quite early next morning, and, when she saw where she was, she began to weep most bitterly, for there was nothing but water on all sides of the large green leaf, and she could in no way reach the land.

Old mother toad was down in the mud, decorating her apartments with bulrushes and yellow buttercups, so as to make it quite gay and tidy to receive her new daughter-in-law. At last, she and her frightful son swam together to the leaf where she had left Thumbelina; they wanted to fetch her pretty cradle, and place it for her in the bridal chamber before she herself was conducted into it. Old mother toad bowed low in the water, and said to her, "Here is my son, he is to be thy husband, and you will dwell together so comfortably down in the mud!"

"Coax, coax, brekke-ke-kex!" was all that her son could say.

Then they took the neat little bed and swam away with it, whilst Thumbelina sat alone on the green leaf, weeping, for she did not like the thought of living with the withered old toad, and having her ugly son for a husband. The little fishes that were swimming to and fro in the water beneath had heard what mother toad had said, so they now put up their heads—they wanted to see the little maid. And when they saw her, they were charmed with her delicate beauty, and it vexed them very much that the hideous old toad should carry her off. No, that should never be! They surrounded the green stalk in the water, whereon rested the water-lily leaf, and gnawed it asunder with their teeth, and then the leaf floated away down the brook, with Thumbelina on it; away, far away, where the old toad could not follow.

Thumbelina sailed past so many places, and the wild birds among the bushes saw her and sang, "Oh, what a sweet little maiden!" On and on, farther and farther, floated the leaf: Thumbelina was on her travels.

A pretty little white butterfly kept fluttering round and round her, and at last settled down on the leaf, for he loved Thumbelina very much, and she was so pleased. There was nothing to trouble her now that she had no fear of the old toad pursuing her, and wherever she sailed everything was so beautiful, for the sun shone down on the water, making it bright as liquid gold. And now she took off her sash, and tied one end of it round the butterfly, fastening the other end firmly into the leaf. On floated the leaf, faster and faster, and Thumbelina with it.

Presently a great cock-chafer came buzzing past; he caught sight of her, and immediately fastening his claw round her slender waist, flew up into a tree with her. But the green leaf still floated down the brook, and the butterfly with it; he was bound to the leaf and could not get loose.

Oh, how terrified was poor Thumbelina when the cock-chafer carried her up into the tree, and how sorry she felt, too, for the darling white butterfly which she had left tied fast to the leaf; she feared that if he could not get away, he would perish of hunger. But the cock-chafer cared nothing for that. He settled with her upon the largest leaf in the tree, gave her some honey from the flowers to eat, and hummed her praises, telling her she was very pretty, although she was not at all like a hen-chafer. And by-and-by all the chafers who lived in that tree came to pay her a visit; they looked at Thumbelina, and one Miss Hen-chafer drew in her feelers, saying, "She has only two legs, how miserable that looks!" "She has no feelers," cried another. "And see how thin and lean her waist is; why, she is just like a human being!" observed a third. "How very, very ugly she is!" at last cried all the lady-chafers in chorus. The chafer who had carried off Thumbelina still could not persuade himself that she was otherwise than pretty, but, as all the rest kept repeating and insisting that she was ugly, he at last began to think they must be in the right, and determined to have nothing more to do with her; she might go wherever she would, for aught he cared, he said. And so the whole swarm flew down from the tree with her, and set her on a daisy; then she wept because she was so ugly that the lady-chafers would not keep company with her, and yet Thumbelina was the prettiest little creature that could be imagined, soft and delicate and transparent as the loveliest rose leaf.

Oh, how terrified was poor Thumbelina

All the summer long poor Thumbelina lived alone in the wide wood. She wove herself a bed of grass-straw, and hung it under a large burdock-leaf which sheltered her from the rain; she dined off the honey from the flowers, and drank from the dew that every morning spangled the leaves and herblets around her. Thus passed the summer and autumn, but then came winter, the cold, long winter. All the birds who had sung so sweetly to her flew away, trees and flowers withered, the large burdock-leaf under which Thumbelina had lived rolled itself up and became a dry, yellow stalk, and Thumbelina was fearfully cold, for her clothes were wearing out, and she herself was so slight and frail, poor little thing! she was nearly frozen to death. It began to snow, and every light flake that fell upon her made her feel as we should if a whole shovelful of snow were thrown upon us, for we are giants in comparison with a little creature only an inch long. She wrapped herself up in a withered leaf, but it gave her no warmth; she shuddered with cold.

Close outside the wood, on the skirt of which Thumbelina had been living, lay a large corn-field, but the corn had been carried away long ago, leaving only the dry, naked stubble standing up from the hard-frozen earth. It was like another wood to Thumbelina, and oh, how she shivered with cold as she made her way through. At last she came past the field mouse's door; for the field-mouse had made herself a little hole under the stubble, and there she dwelt snugly and comfortably, having a room full of corn, and a neat kitchen and store-chamber besides. And poor Thumbelina must now play the beggar-girl; she stood at the door and begged for a little piece of a barley-corn, for she had had nothing to eat during two whole days.

PLATE 4.
She stood at the door and begged for a piece
of barley-corn

"Thou poor little thing!" said the field-mouse, who was indeed a thoroughly good-natured old creature, "come into my warm room and dine with me."

And as she soon took a great liking to Thumbelina, she proposed to her to stay. "You may dwell with me all the winter if you will, but keep my room clean and neat, and tell me stories, for I love stories dearly."

And Thumbelina did all that the kind old field-mouse required of her, and was made very comfortable in her new abode.

"We shall have a visitor presently," observed the field mouse; "my next-door neighbor comes to see me once every week. He is better off than I am, has large rooms in his house, and wears a coat of such beautiful black velvet. It would be a capital thing for

"Thou poor little thing!" said the field-mouse

you if you could secure him for your husband, but unfortunately he is blind, he cannot see you. You must tell him the prettiest stories you know."

But Thumbelina did not care at all about pleasing their neighbor Mr. Mole, nor did she wish to marry him. He came and paid a visit in his black-velvet suit, he was so rich and so learned, and the field-mouse declared his domestic offices were twenty times larger than hers, but the sun and the pretty flowers he could not endure, he was always abusing them, though he had never seen either. Thumbelina was called upon to sing for his amusement, and by the time she had sung "Lady-bird, lady-bird, fly away home!" and "The Friar of Orders Grey," the mole had quite fallen in love with her through the charm of her sweet voice; however, he said nothing, he was such a prudent, cautious animal.

He had just been digging a long passage through the earth from their house to his, and he now gave permission to the field-mouse and Thumbelina to walk in it as often as they liked; however, he bade them not be afraid of the dead bird that lay in the passage; it was a whole bird, with beak and feathers entire, and therefore he supposed it must have died quite lately, at the beginning of the winter, and had been buried just in the place where he had dug his passage.

The mole took a piece of tinder, which shines like fire in the dark, in his mouth, and went on first to light his friends through the long dark passage, and when they came to the place where the dead bird lay, he thrust his broad nose up against the ceiling and pushed up the earth, so as to make a great hole for the light to come through. In the midst of the floor lay a swallow, his wings clinging firmly to his sides, his head and legs drawn under the feathers;

the poor bird had evidently died of cold. Thumbelina felt so very sorry, for she loved all the little birds, who had sung and chirped so merrily to her the whole summer long; but the mole kicked it with his short legs, saying, "Here's a fine end to all its whistling! a miserable thing it must be to be born a bird. None of my children will be birds, that's a comfort! Such creatures have nothing but their 'quivit,' and must be starved to death in the winter."

"Yes, indeed, a sensible animal like you may well say so," returned the field-mouse; "what has the bird got by all his chirping and chirruping? when winter comes it must starve and freeze; and it is such a great creature too!"

Thumbelina said nothing, but when the two others had turned their backs upon the bird, she bent over it, smoothed down the feathers that covered its head, and kissed the closed eyes. "Perhaps it was this one that sang so delightfully to me in the summer-time," thought she; "how much pleasure it has given me, the dear, dear bird!"

The mole now stopped up the hole through which the daylight had pierced, and then followed the ladies home. But Thumbelina could not sleep that night, so she got out of her bed, and wove a carpet out of hay, and then went out and spread it round the dead bird; she also fetched some soft cotton from the field-mouse's room, which she laid over the bird, that it might be warm amid the cold earth.

"Farewell, thou dear bird," said she; "farewell, and thanks for thy beautiful song in the summer-time, when all the trees were green, and the sun shone so warmly upon us!" And she pressed her head against the bird's breast, but was terrified to feel something beating within it. It was the bird's heart. The bird was not dead; it had lain in a swoon, and now that it was warmer its life returned.

Every autumn all the swallows fly away to warm countries; but if one of them linger behind, it freezes and falls down as though dead, and the cold snow covers it.

Thumbelina trembled with fright, for the bird was very large compared with her, who was only an inch in length. However, she took courage, laid the cotton more closely round the poor swallow, and fetching a leaf which had served herself as a coverlet, spread it over the bird's head.

The next night she stole out again, and found that the bird's life had quite returned, though it was so feeble that only for one short moment could it open its eyes to look at Thumbelina, who stood by with a piece of tinder in her hand—she had no other lantern.

"Thanks to thee, thou sweet little child!" said the sick swallow. "I feel delightfully warm now; soon I shall recover my strength, and be able to fly again, out in the warm sunshine."

"Oh, no," she replied, "it is too cold without, it snows and freezes! Thou must stay in thy warm bed; I will take care of thee."

She brought the swallow water in a flower-petal and he drank, and then he told her how he had torn one of his wings in a thorn bush, and therefore could not fly fast enough to keep up with the other swallows who were all migrating to the warm countries. He had at last fallen to the earth, and more than that he could not remember; he did not at all know how he had got underground.

However, underground he remained all the winter long, and Thumbelina was kind to him, and loved him dearly, but she never said a word about him either to the mole or the field-mouse, for she knew they could not endure the poor swallow.

As soon as the spring came and the sun's warmth had penetrated the earth, the swallow said farewell to Thumbelina, and she opened for him the covering of earth which the mole had thrown back before. The sun shone in upon them so deliciously, and the swallow asked whether she would not go with him; she might sit upon his back, and then they would fly together far out into the greenwood. But Thumbelina knew it would vex the old field-mouse if she were to leave her.

"No, I cannot, I must not go," said Thumbelina.

"Fare thee well, then, thou good and pretty maiden," said the swallow, and away he flew into the sunshine. Thumbelina looked after him and the tears came into her eyes, for she loved the poor swallow so much.

"Quivit, quivit," sang the bird, as he flew into the greenwood. And Thumbelina was now sad indeed. She was not allowed to go out into the warm sunshine; the wheat that had been sown in the field above the field-mouse's house grew up so high that it seemed a perfect forest to the poor little damsel who was only an inch in stature.

"This summer you must work at getting your wedding clothes ready," said the field-mouse, for their neighbor, the blind dull mole in the black-velvet suit had now made his proposals in form to Thumbelina. "You shall have worsted and linen in plenty; you shall be well provided with all manner of clothes and furniture before you become the mole's wife." So Thumbelina was obliged to work hard at the distaff, and the field-mouse hired four spiders to spin and weave night and day. Every evening came the mole, and always began to talk about the summer soon coming to an end, and that then, when the sun would no longer shine so warmly, scorching the earth till it was as dry as a stone, yes, then, his nuptials with Thumbelina should take place. But this sort of conversation did not please her at all; she was thoroughly wearied of his dullness and his prating. Every morning when the sun rose, and every evening when it set, she used to steal out at the door, and when the wind blew the tops of the corn aside, so that she could see the blue sky through the opening, she thought how bright and beautiful it was out here, and wished most fervently to see the dear swallow once more; but he never came, he must have been flying far away in the beautiful greenwood.

Autumn came, and Thumbelina's wedding clothes were ready.

"Four weeks more, and you shall be married!" said the field-mouse. But Thumbelina wept, and said she would not marry the dull mole.

"Fiddlestick!" exclaimed the field-mouse; "don't be obstinate, child, or I shall bite thee with my white teeth! Is he not handsome, pray? Why, the Queen has not got such a black-velvet dress as he wears! And isn't he rich? rich both in kitchens and cellars? Be thankful to get such a husband!"

So Thumbelina must be married. The day fixed had arrived, the mole had already come to fetch his bride, and she must dwell with him, deep under the earth, never again to come out into the warm sunshine which she loved so much, and which he could not endure. The poor child was in despair at the thought that she must now bid farewell to the beautiful sun of which she had at least been allowed to catch a glimpse every now and then while she lived with the field-mouse.

"Farewell, thou glorious sun!" she cried, throwing her arms up into the air, and she walked on a little way beyond the field-mouse's door; the corn was already reaped, and only the dry stubble surrounded her. "Farewell, farewell!" repeated she, as she clasped her tiny arms round a little red flower that grew there. "Greet the dear swallow from me, if thou shouldst see him."

"Quivit! quivit!"—there was a fluttering of wings just over her head; she looked up, and behold! the little swallow was flying past. And how pleased he was when he perceived Thumbelina! She told how that she had been obliged to accept the disagreeable mole as a husband, and that she would have to dwell deep underground where the sun never pierced. And she could not help weeping as she spoke.

"The cold winter will soon be here!" said the swallow; "I shall fly far away to the warm countries. Wilt thou go with me? Thou canst sit on my back, and tie thyself firmly to me with thy sash, and thus we shall fly away from the stupid mole and his dark room, far away over the mountains to those countries where the sun shines so brightly, where it is always summer, and flowers blossom all the year round. Come and fly with me, thou sweet little Thumbelina, who didst save my life when I lay frozen in the dark cellars of the earth!"

"Yes, I will go with thee!" said Thumbelina. And she seated herself on the bird's back, her feet resting on the outspread wings, and tied her girdle firmly round one of the strongest feathers, and then the swallow soared high into the air, and flew away over forest and over lake, over mountains whose crests are covered with snow all the year round. How Thumbelina shivered as she breathed the keen frosty air! However, she soon crept down under the bird's warm feathers, her head still peering forth, eager to behold all the glory and beauty beneath her. At last they reached the warm countries. There the sun shone far more brightly than in her native clime. The heavens seemed twice as high, and twice as blue; and ranged along the sloping hills grew, in rich luxuriance, the loveliest green and purple grapes. Citrons and melons were seen in the groves, the fragrance of myrtles and balsams filled the air, and by the wayside gamboled groups of pretty merry children, chasing large bright-winged butterflies.

But the swallow did not rest here; still he flew on; and still the scene seemed to grow more and more beautiful. Near a calm, blue lake, overhung by lofty trees, stood a half-ruined palace of white marble, built in times long past; vine-wreaths trailed up the long slender pillars, and on the capitals, among the green leaves and waving tendrils, many a swallow had built his nest, and one of these nests belonged to the swallow on whose back Thumbelina was riding.

"This is my house," said the swallow, "but if thou wouldst rather choose for thyself one of the splendid flowers growing beneath us, I will take thee there, and thou shalt make thy home in the loveliest of them all."

"That will be charming!" exclaimed she, clapping her tiny hands.

On the green turf beneath there lay the fragments of a white marble column which had fallen to the ground, and around these fragments twined some beautiful large white flowers. The swallow flew down with Thumbelina, and set her on one of the broad petals. But what was her surprise when she saw sitting in the very heart of the flower a little mannikin, fair and transparent

PLATE 5.
"Yes! I will go with thee," said Thumbelina, and
she seated herself on the bird's back

as though he were made of glass! wearing the prettiest gold crown on his head, and the brightest, most delicate wings on his shoulders, yet scarcely one whit larger than Thumbelina herself. He was the spirit of the flower. In every blossom there dwelt one such faëry youth or maiden, but this one was the king of all these flower-spirits.

"Oh, how handsome he is, this king!" whispered Thumbelina to the swallow. The faëry prince was quite startled at the sudden descent of the swallow, who was a sort of giant compared with him; but when he saw Thumbelina he was delighted, for she was the very loveliest maiden he had ever seen. So he took his gold crown off his own head and set it upon hers, asked her name, and whether she would be his bride, and reign as queen over all

That was the greatest of pleasures

the flower-spirits. This, you see, was quite a different bridegroom from the son of the ugly old toad, or the blind mole with his black-velvet coat. So Thumbelina replied "Yes" to the beautiful prince, and then the lady and gentlemen faëries came out, each from a separate flower, to pay their homage to Thumbelina; so gracefully and courteously they paid their homage: and every one of them brought her a present.

But the best of all the presents was a pair of transparent wings; they were fastened on Thumbelina's shoulders, and enabled her to fly from flower to flower. That was the greatest of pleasures; and the little swallow sat in his nest above and sang to her his sweetest song; in his heart, however, he was very sad, for he loved Thumbelina, and would have wished never to part from her.

"Thou shalt no longer be called Thumbelina," said the king of flowers to her, "for it is not a pretty name, and thou art so lovely! We will call thee Maia."

"Farewell! farewell!" sang the swallow, and away he flew from the warm countries, far away back to Denmark. There he had a little nest just over the window of the man who writes stories for children. "Quivit, quivit, quivit!" he sang to him, and from him we have learned this history.

They carried the mirror from place to place

THE SNOW QUEEN
IN SEVEN PARTS

✤ PART THE FIRST ✤

WHICH TREATS OF THE MIRROR AND ITS FRAGMENTS

LISTEN! WE ARE BEGINNING OUR STORY! WHEN WE ARRIVE AT the end of it we shall, it is to be hoped, know more than we do now. There was once a magician! a wicked magician!! a most wicked magician!!! Great was his delight at having constructed a mirror possessing this peculiarity, viz.:—that everything good and beautiful, when reflected in it, shrank up almost to nothing, whilst those things that were ugly and useless were magnified, and made to appear ten times worse than before. The loveliest landscapes reflected in this mirror looked like boiled spinach; and the handsomest persons appeared odious, or as if standing upon their heads, their features being so distorted that their friends could never have recognized them. Moreover, if one of them had a freckle, he might be sure that it would seem to spread over the nose and mouth; and if a good or pious thought glanced across his mind, a wrinkle was seen in the mirror. All this the magician thought highly entertaining, and he chuckled with delight at his own clever invention. Those who frequented the school of magic where he taught spread abroad the fame of this wonderful mirror, and declared that by its means the world and its inhabitants might be seen now for the first time as they really were. They carried the mirror from place to place, till at last there was no country nor person that had not been misrepresented in it. Its admirers now must needs fly up to the sky with it, to see if they could carry on their sport even there. But the higher they flew the more wrinkled did the mirror become; they could scarcely hold it together. They flew on and on, higher and higher, till at last the mirror trembled so fearfully that it escaped from their hands, and fell to the earth, breaking into millions, billions, and trillions of pieces. And then it caused far greater unhappiness than before, for fragments of it, scarcely so large as a grain of sand, would be flying about in the air, and sometimes get into people's eyes, causing them to view everything the wrong way, or to have eyes only for what

He chuckled with delight

was perverted and corrupt; each little fragment having retained the peculiar properties of the entire mirror. Some people were so unfortunate as to receive a little splinter into their hearts—that was terrible! The heart became cold and hard, like a lump of ice. Some pieces were large enough to be used as window panes, but it was of no use to look at one's friends through such panes as those. Other fragments were made into spectacles, and then what trouble people had with setting and re-setting them!

The wicked magician was greatly amused with all this, and he laughed till his sides ached.

There are still some little splinters of this mischievous mirror flying about in the air. We shall hear more about them very soon.

✣ PART THE SECOND ✣
A LITTLE BOY AND A LITTLE GIRL

In a large town, where there are so many houses and inhabitants that there is not room enough for all the people to possess a little garden of their own, and therefore many are obliged to content themselves with keeping a few plants in pots, there dwelt two poor children, whose garden was somewhat larger than a flower-pot. They were not brother and sister, but they loved each other as much as if they had been, and their parents lived in two attics exactly opposite. The roof of one neighbor's house nearly joined the other, the gutter ran along between, and there was in each roof a little window, so that you could stride across the gutter from one window to the other. The parents of each child had a large wooden box in which grew herbs for kitchen use, and they had placed these boxes upon the gutter, so near that they almost touched each other. A beautiful little rose-tree grew in each box, scarlet runners entwined their long shoots over the windows, and, uniting with the branches of the rose-trees, formed a flowery arch across the street. The boxes were very high, and the children knew that they might not climb over them, but they often obtained leave to sit on their little stools, under the rose-trees, and thus they passed many a delightful hour.

But when winter came there was an end to these pleasures. The windows were often quite frozen over, and then they heated halfpence on the stove, held the warm copper against the frozen pane, and thus made a little round peep-hole, behind which would sparkle a bright gentle eye, one from each window.

The little boy was called Kay, the little girl's name was Gerda. In summer-time they could get out of window and jump over to each other; but in winter there were stairs to run down, and stairs to run up, and sometimes the wind roared, and the snow fell without-doors.

"Those are the white bees swarming there!" said the old grandmother.

"Have they a Queen bee?" asked the little boy, for he knew that the real bees have one.

"They have," said the grandmother. "She flies yonder where they swarm so thickly; she is the largest of them, and never remains upon the earth, but flies up again into the black cloud. Sometimes on a winter's night she flies through the streets of the town, and breathes with her frosty breath upon the windows, and then they are covered with strange and beautiful forms, like trees and flowers."

"Yes, I have seen them!" said both the children—they knew that this was true.

"Can the Snow Queen come in here?" asked the little girl.

"If she do come in," said the boy, "I will put her on the warm stove and then she will melt."

And the grandmother stroked his hair and told him some stories.

That same evening, after little Kay had gone home, and was half undressed, he crept upon the chair by the window and peeped through the little round hole. Just then a few snow-flakes fell outside, and one, the largest of them, remained lying on the edge of one of the flower-pots. The snow-flake appeared larger and larger, and at last took the form of a lady dressed in the finest white crape, her attire being composed of millions of star-like particles. She was exquisitely fair and delicate, but entirely of ice, glittering, dazzling ice; her eyes gleamed like two bright stars, but there was no rest or repose in them. She nodded at the window, and beckoned with her hand. The little boy was frightened and jumped down from the chair; he then fancied he saw a large bird fly past the window.

There was a clear frost next day, and soon afterwards came spring—the trees and flowers budded, the swallows built their nests, the windows were opened, and the little children sat once more in their little garden upon the gutter that ran along the roofs of the houses.

The roses blossomed beautifully that summer, and the little girl had learned a hymn in which there was something about roses; it reminded her of her own. So she sang it to the little boy, and he sang it with her.

"Our roses bloom and fade away,
Our Infant Lord abides alway;
May we be blessed His face to see,
And ever little children be!"

And the little ones held each other by the hand, kissed the roses, and looked up into the blue sky, talking away all the time. What glorious summer days were those! how delightful it was to sit under those rose-trees which seemed as if they never intended to leave off blossoming! One day Kay and Gerda were sitting looking at their picture-book full of birds and animals, when suddenly—the clock on the old church tower was just striking five—Kay exclaimed, "Oh, dear! what was that shooting pain in my heart: and now again, something has certainly got into my eye!"

The little girl turned and looked at him. He winked his eyes; no, there was nothing to be seen.

"I believe it is gone," said he; but gone it was not. It was one of those glass splinters from the Magic Mirror, the wicked glass which made everything great and good reflected in it to appear little and hateful, and which magnified everything ugly and mean. Poor Kay had also received a splinter in his heart; it would now become hard and cold like a lump of ice. He felt the pain no longer, but the splinter was there.

"Why do you cry?" asked he; "you look so ugly when you cry! there is nothing the matter with me. Fie!" exclaimed he again, "this rose has an insect in it, and just look at this! After all, they are ugly roses! and it is an ugly box they grow in!" then he kicked the box, and tore off the roses.

"O Kay, what are you doing?" cried the little girl, but when he saw how it grieved her, he tore off another rose, and jumped down through his own window, away from his once dear little Gerda.

Ever afterwards when she brought forward the picture-book, he called it a baby's book, and when her grandmother told stories, he interrupted her with a "but," and sometimes, whenever he could manage it, he would get behind her, put on her spectacles, and speak just as she did; he did this in a very droll manner, and so people laughed at him. Very soon he could mimic everybody in the street. All that was singular and awkward about them could Kay imitate, and his neighbors said, "What a remarkable head that boy has!" But no, it was the glass splinter which had fallen into his eye, the glass splinter which had pierced into his heart—it was these which made him regardless whose feelings he wounded, and even made him tease the little Gerda who loves him so fondly.

His games were now quite different from what they used to be, they were so rational! One winter's day when it was snowing, he came out with a large burning-glass in his hand, and holding up the skirts of his blue coat let the snow-flakes fall upon them. "Now look through the glass, Gerda!" said he, returning to the house. Every snow-flake seemed much larger, and resembled a splendid flower, or a star with ten points; they were quite beautiful. "See, how curious!" said Kay, "these are far more interesting than real flowers, there is not a single blemish in them; they would be quite perfect if only they did not melt."

Soon after this Kay came in again, with thick gloves on his hands, and his sledge slung across his back. He called out to

Gerda, "I have got leave to drive on the great square where the other boys play!" and away he went.

The boldest boys in the square used to fasten their sledges firmly to the wagons of the country people, and thus drive a good way along with them; this they thought particularly pleasant. Whilst they were in the midst of their play, a large sledge painted white passed by; in it sat a person wrapped in a rough white fur, and wearing a rough white cap. When the sledge had driven twice round the square, Kay bound to it his little sledge, and was carried on with it. On they went, faster and faster, into the next street. The person who drove the large sledge turned round and nodded kindly to Kay, just as if they had been old acquaintances, and every time Kay was going to loose his little sledge turned and nodded again, as if to signify that he must stay. So Kay sat still, and they passed through the gates of the town. Then the snow began to fall so thickly that the little boy could not see his own hand, but he was still carried on. He tried hastily to unloose the cords and free himself from the large sledge, but it was of no use; his little carriage could not be unfastened, and glided on swift as the wind. Then he cried out as loud as he could, but no one heard him, the snow fell and the sledge flew; every now and then it made a spring as if driving over hedges and ditches. He was very much frightened; he would have repeated "Our Father," but he could remember nothing but the multiplication table.

The snow-flakes seemed larger and larger, at last they looked like great white fowls. All at once they fell aside, the large sledge stopped, and the person who drove it arose from the seat. He saw that the cap and coat were entirely of snow, that it was a lady, tall and slender, and dazzlingly white—it was the Snow Queen!

"We have driven fast!" said she, "but no one likes to be frozen; creep under my bear-skin," and she seated him in the sledge by her side, and spread her cloak around him—he felt as if he were sinking into a drift of snow.

"Are you still cold?" asked she, and then she kissed his brow. Oh! her kiss was colder than ice. It went to his heart, although that was half frozen already; he thought he should die. It was, however, only for a moment; directly afterwards he was quite well, and no longer felt the intense cold around.

"My sledge! do not forget my sledge!"—he thought first of that—it was fastened to one of the white fowls which flew behind with it on his back. The Snow Queen kissed Kay again, and he entirely forgot little Gerda, her grandmother, and all at home.

"Now you must have no more kisses!" said she, "else I should kiss thee to death."

Kay looked at her, she was so beautiful; a more intelligent, more lovely countenance, he could not imagine; she no longer appeared to him ice, cold ice as at the time when she sat outside the window and beckoned to him; in his eyes she was perfect; he felt no fear. He told her how well he could reckon in his head, even fractions; that he knew the number of square miles of every country, and the number of the inhabitants contained in different towns. She smiled, and then it occurred to him that, after all, he did not yet know so very much. He looked up into the wide, wide space, and she flew with him high up into the black cloud while the storm was raging; it seemed now to Kay as though singing songs of olden time.

They flew over woods and over lakes, over sea and over land; beneath them the cold wind whistled, the wolves howled, the snow glittered, and the black crow flew cawing over the plain, whilst above them shone the moon, so clear and tranquil.

Thus did Kay spend the long, long winter night; all day he slept at the feet of the Snow Queen.

❋ PART THE THIRD ❋

THE ENCHANTED FLOWER-GARDEN

But how fared it with little Gerda when Kay never re turned? Where could he be? No one knew, no one could give any account of him. The boy said that they had seen him fasten his sledge to another larger and very handsome one which had driven into the street, and thence through the gates of the town. No one knew where he was, and many were the tears that were shed; little Gerda wept much and long, for the boys said he must be dead, he must have been drowned in the river that flowed not far from the town. Oh, how long and dismal the winter days were now! At last came the spring, with its warm sunshine.

"Alas, Kay is dead and gone," said little Gerda.

"That I do not believe," said the sunshine.

"He is dead and gone," said she to the swallows.

"That we do not believe," returned they, and at last little Gerda herself did not believe it.

"I will put on my new red shoes," said she one morning, "those which Kay has never seen, and then I will go down to the river and ask after him."

It was quite early. She kissed her old grandmother, who was still sleeping, put on her red shoes, and went alone through the gates of the town towards the river.

"Is it true," said she, "that thou hast taken my little playfellow away? I will give thee my red shoes if thou wilt restore him to me!"

And the wavelets of the river flowed towards her in a manner which she fancied was unusual; she fancied that they intended to accept her offer, so she took off her red shoes—though she prized them more than anything else she possessed—and threw them into the stream; but they fell near the shore, and the little waves bore them back to her, as though they would not take from her what she most prized, as they had not got little Kay. However, she thought she had not thrown the shoes far enough, so she stepped into a little boat which lay among the reeds by the shore, and, standing at the farthest end of it, threw them from thence into the water. The boat was not fastened, and her movements in it caused it to glide away from the shore. She saw this, and hastened to get out, but by the time she reached the other end of the boat it was more than a yard distant from the land; she could not escape, and the boat glided on.

Little Gerda was much frightened and began to cry, but no one besides the sparrows heard her, and they could not carry her back to the land; however, they flew along the banks, and sang, as if to comfort her, "Here we are, here we are!" The boat followed the stream. Little Gerda sat in it quite still; her red shoes floated behind her, but they could not overtake the boat, which glided along faster than they did.

Beautiful were the shores of that river; lovely flowers, stately old trees, and bright green hills dotted with sheep and cows, were seen in abundance, but not a single human being.

"Perhaps the river may bear me to my dear Kay," thought Gerda, and then she became more cheerful, and amused herself for hours with looking at the lovely country around her. At last she glided past a large cherry-garden, wherein stood a little cottage with thatched roof and curious red and blue windows; two wooden soldiers stood at the door, who presented arms when they saw the little vessel approach.

Gerda called to them, thinking that they were alive, but they, naturally enough, made no answer. She came close up to them, for the stream drifted the boat to the land.

Gerda called still louder, whereupon an old lady came out of the house, supporting herself on a crutch; she wore a large hat, with most beautiful flowers painted on it.

"Thou poor little child!" said the old woman, "the mighty flowing river has indeed borne thee a long, long way," and she walked right into the water, seized the boat with her crutch, drew it to land, and took out the little girl.

Gerda was glad to be on dry land again, although she was a little afraid of the strange old lady.

She wore a large hat, with most beautiful
flowers painted on it

"Come and tell me who thou art, and how thou earnest hither," said she.

And Gerda told her all, and the old lady shook her head, and said, "Hem! hem!" And when Gerda asked if she had seen little Kay, the lady said that he had not arrived there yet, but that he would be sure to come soon, and that in the mean time Gerda must not be sad; that she might stay with her, might eat her cherries, and look at her flowers, which were prettier than any picture-book, and could each tell her a story.

She then took Gerda by the hand; they went together into the cottage, and the old lady shut the door. The windows were very high and their panes of different colored glass, red, blue, and yellow, so that when the bright daylight streamed through them, various and beautiful were the hues reflected upon the room. Upon a table in the center was placed a plate of very fine cherries, and of these Gerda was allowed to eat as many as she liked. And whilst she was eating them, the old dame combed her hair with a golden comb, and the bright flaxen ringlets fell on each side of her pretty, gentle face, which looked as round and as fresh as a rose.

"I have long wished for such a dear little girl," said the old lady. "We shall see if we cannot live very happily together." And, as she combed little Gerda's hair, the child thought less and less of her foster-brother Kay, for the old lady was an enchantress. She did not, however, practice magic for the sake of mischief, but merely for her own amusement. And now she wished very much to keep little Gerda, to live with her; so, fearing that if Gerda saw her roses, she would be reminded of her own flowers and of little Kay, and that then she might run away, she went out into the garden, and extended her crutch over all her rose-bushes, upon which, although they were full of leaves and blossoms, they immediately sank into the black earth, and no one would have guessed that such plants had ever grown there.

Then she led Gerda into this flower-garden. Oh how beautiful and how fragrant it was! Flowers of all seasons and all climes grew there in fullness of beauty—certainly no picture-book could be compared with it. Gerda bounded with delight, and played among the flowers till the sun set behind the tall cherry-trees; after which a pretty little bed, with crimson silk cushions, stuffed with blue violet leaves, was prepared for her, and here she slept so sweetly and had such dreams as a queen might have on her bridal eve.

The next day she again played among the flowers in the warm sunshine, and many more days were spent in the same manner. Gerda knew every flower in the garden, but, numerous as they were, it seemed to her that one was wanting, she could not tell which. She was sitting one day, looking at her hostess's hat, which had flowers painted on it, and, behold, the loveliest among them was a rose! The old lady had entirely forgotten the painted rose on her hat, when she made the real roses to disappear from her garden and sink into the ground. This is often the case when things are done hastily.

"What," cried Gerda, "are there no roses in the garden?" And she ran from one bed to another, sought and sought again, but no rose was to be found. She sat down and wept, and it so chanced that her tears fell on a spot where a rose-tree had formerly stood, and as soon as her warm tears had moistened the earth, the bush shot up anew, as fresh and as blooming as it was before it had sunk into the ground; and Gerda threw her arms around it, kissed

Gerda knew every flower in the garden

the blossoms, and immediately recalled to memory the beautiful roses at home, and her little playfellow Kay. "Oh, how could I stay here so long!" exclaimed the little maiden. "I left my home to seek for Kay. Do you know where he is?" she asked of the roses; "think you that he is dead?"

"Dead he is not," said the roses. "We have been down in the earth; the dead are there, but not Kay."

"I thank you," said little Gerda, and she went to the other flowers, bent low over their cups, and asked, "Know you not where little Kay is?"

But every flower stood in the sunshine dreaming its own little tale. They related their stories to Gerda, but none of them knew anything of Kay.

"And what think you?" said the tiger-lily.

"Listen to the drums beating, boom! boom! They have but two notes, always boom! boom! Listen to the dirge the women are singing! Listen to the chorus of priests! Enveloped in her long red robes stands the Hindoo wife on the funeral pile; the flames blaze around her and her dead husband, but the Hindoo wife thinks not of the dead. She thinks only of the living, and the anguish which consumes her spirit is keener than the fire which will soon reduce her body to ashes. Can the flame of the heart expire amid the flames of the funeral pile?"

"I do not understand that at all!" said little Gerda.

"That is my tale!" said the tiger-lily.

"What says the convolvulus?"

"Hanging over a narrow mountain causeway, behold an ancient, baronial castle. Thick evergreens grow amongst the time stained walls, their leafy branches entwine about the balcony, and there stands a beautiful maiden; she bends over the balustrades and fixes her eyes with eager expectation on the road winding beneath. The rose hangs not fresher and lovelier on its stem than she; the apple-blossom which the wind threatens every moment to tear from its branch is not more fragile and trembling. Listen to the rustling of her rich silken robe! Listen to her half whispered words, 'He comes not yet.' "

"Is it Kay you mean?" asked little Gerda.

"I do but tell you my tale—my dream," replied the convolvulus.

"What says the little snowdrop?"

"Between two trees hangs a swing. Two pretty little maidens, their dress as white as snow, and long green ribbands fluttering from their hats, sit and swing themselves in it. Their brother stands up in the swing, he has thrown his arms round the ropes to keep himself steady, for in one hand he holds a little cup, in the other a pipe made of clay; he is blowing soap bubbles. The swing moves and the bubbles fly upwards with bright, ever-changing colors; the last hovers on the edge of the pipe, and moves with the wind. The swing is still in motion, and the little black dog, almost as light as the soap bubbles, rises on his hind feet and tries to get into the swing also; away goes the swing, the dog falls, is out of temper, and barks; he is laughed at, and the bubbles burst. A swinging board, a frothy, fleeting image is my song."

"What you describe may be all very pretty, but you speak so mournfully, and there is nothing about Kay."

"What say the hyacinths?"

"There were three fair sisters, transparent and delicate they were; the kirtle of the one was red, that of the second blue, of the third pure white; hand in hand they danced in the moonlight

PLATE 6.
The swing moves and the bubbles fly upward with
bright, ever-changing colors

beside the quiet lake; they were not fairies, but daughters of men. Sweet was the fragrance when the maidens vanished into the wood; the fragrance grew stronger; three biers, whereon lay the fair sisters, glided out from the depths of the wood, and floated upon the lake; the glow-worms flew shining around like little hovering lamps. Sleep the dancing maidens, or are they dead? The odor from the flowers tells us they are corpses, the evening bells peal out their dirge."

"You make me quite sad," said little Gerda. "Your fragrance is so strong I cannot help thinking of the dead maidens. Alas! and is little Kay dead? The roses have been under the earth, and they say no!"

"Ding dong! ding dong!" rang the hyacinth bells. "We toll not for little Kay, we know him not! We do but sing our own song, the only one we know!"

And Gerda went to the buttercup, which shone so brightly from among her smooth green leaves.

"Thou art like a little bright sun," said Gerda; "tell me, if thou canst, where I may find my playfellow."

And the buttercup glittered so brightly, and looked at Gerda. What song could the buttercup sing? Neither was hers about Kay. "One bright spring morning, the sun shone warmly upon a little court-yard. The bright beams streamed down the white walls of a neighboring house, and close by grew the first yellow flower of spring, glittering like gold in the warm sunshine. An old grandmother sat without in her arm-chair, her grand-daughter, a pretty, lowly maiden, had just returned home from a short visit; she kissed her grand mother; there was gold, pure gold, in that loving kiss:

"Gold was the flower!
Gold the fresh, bright, morning hour!"

"That is my little story," said the buttercup.

"My poor old grandmother!" sighed Gerda; "yes, she must be wishing for me, just as she wished for little Kay. But I shall soon go home again, and take Kay with me. It is of no use to ask the flowers about him; they only know their own song, they can give me no information." And she folded her little frock round her, that she might run the faster; but, in jumping over the narcissus, it caught her foot, as if wishing to stop her, so she turned and looked at the tall yellow flower, "Have you any news to give me?" She bent over the narcissus, waiting for an answer.

And what said the narcissus?

"I can look at myself!—I can see myself! Oh, how sweet is my fragrance!" Up in the little attic-chamber stands a little dancer. She rests sometimes on one leg, sometimes on two. She has trampled the whole world under her feet; she is nothing but an illusion. She pours water from a tea-pot upon a piece of cloth she holds in her hand—it is her bodice; cleanliness is a fine thing! Her white dress hangs on the hook, that has also been washed by the water from the tea-pot, and dried on the roof of the house. She puts it on, and wraps a saffron-colored handkerchief round her neck; it makes the dress look all the whiter. With one leg extended, there she stands, as though on a stalk. "I can look at myself!—I see myself!"

"I don't care if you do!" said Gerda. "You need not have told me that!" and away she ran to the end of the garden.

The gate was closed, but she pressed upon the rusty lock till it broke. The gate sprang open, and little Gerda, with bare feet, ran out into the wide world. Three times she looked back, there was no one following her; she ran till she could run no longer, and then sat down to rest upon a large stone. Casting a glance around, she saw that the summer was past, that it was now late in the autumn. Of course, she had not remarked this in the enchanted garden, where there were sunshine and flowers all the year round.

"How long I must have stayed there!" said little Gerda. "So, it is now autumn! Well, then, there is no time to lose!" and she rose to pursue her way.

Oh, how sore and weary were her little feet; and all around looked so cold and barren. The long willow-leaves had already turned yellow, and the dew trickled down from them like water. The leaves fell off the trees, one by one; the sloe alone bore fruit, and its berries were so sharp and bitter! Cold, and grey, and sad seemed the world to her that day.

PART THE FOURTH

THE PRINCE AND THE PRINCESS

Gerda was again obliged to stop and take rest. Suddenly a large raven hopped upon the snow in front of her, saying, "Caw!— Caw!—Good-day!—Good-day!" He sat for some time on the withered branch of a tree just opposite, eyeing the little maiden, and wagging his head, and he now came forward to make acquaintance and to ask her whither she was going all alone. That word "alone" Gerda understood right well—she felt how sad a meaning it has. She told the raven the history of her life and fortunes, and asked if he had seen Kay.

Suddenly a large raven hopped upon the snow in front of her

HANS CHRISTIAN ANDERSEN

And the raven nodded his head, half doubtfully, and said, "That is possible—possible."

"Do you think so?" exclaimed the little girl, and she kissed the raven so vehemently that it is a wonder she did not squeeze him to death.

"More moderately!—moderately!" said the raven. "I think I know. I think it may be little Kay; but he has certainly forsaken thee for the princess."

"Dwells he with a princess?" asked Gerda.

"Listen to me," said the raven, "but it is so difficult to speak your language! Do you understand Ravenish? If so, I can tell you much better."

"No! I have never learned Ravenish," said Gerda, "but my grandmother knew it, and Pye-language also. Oh, how I wish I had learned it!"

"Never mind," said the raven, "I will relate my story in the best manner I can, though bad will be the best"; and he told all he knew.

"In the kingdom wherein we are now sitting, there dwells a princess, a most uncommonly clever princess. All the newspapers in the world has she read, and forgotten them again, so clever is she. It is not long since she ascended the throne, which I have heard is not quite so agreeable a situation as one would fancy; and immediately after she began to sing a new song, the burden of which was this, 'Why should I not marry me?' 'There is some sense in this song!' said she, and she determined she would marry, but at the same time declared that the man whom she would choose must be able to answer sensibly whenever people spoke to him, and must be good for something else besides merely looking grand and stately. The ladies of the court were then all drummed together, in order to be informed of her intentions, whereupon they were highly delighted, and one exclaimed, 'That is just what I wish'; and another, that she had lately been thinking of the very same thing. Believe me," continued the raven, "every word I say is true, for I have a tame beloved who hops at pleasure about the palace, and she has told me all this."

Of course the "beloved" was also a raven, for birds of a feather flock together.

"Proclamations, adorned with borders of hearts, were immediately issued, wherein, after enumerating the style and titles of the princess, it was set forth that every well-favored youth was free to go to the palace and converse with the princess, and that whoever should speak in such wise as showed that he felt himself at home, there would be the one the princess would choose for her husband.

"Yes, indeed," continued the raven, "you may believe me; all this is as true as that I sit here. The people all crowded to the palace; there was famous pressing and squeezing; but it was all of no use, either the first or the second day; the young men could speak well enough while they were outside the palace gates, but when they entered, and saw the royal guard in silver uniform, and the lackeys on the staircase in gold, and the spacious saloon, all lighted up, they were quite confounded. They stood before the throne where the princess sat, and when she spoke to them, they could only repeat the last word she had uttered, which, you know, it was not particularly interesting for her to hear over again. It was just as though they had been struck dumb the moment they entered the palace, for as soon as they got out, they could talk fast enough. There was a regular procession constantly moving from the gates of the town to the gates of the palace. I was there, and saw it with my own eyes," said the raven. "They grew both hungry and thirsty whilst waiting at the palace, but no one could get even so much as a glass of water; to be sure, some of them, wiser than the rest, had brought with them slices of bread and butter, but none would give any to his neighbor, for he thought to himself, 'Let him look hungry, and then the princess will be sure not to choose him.' "

"But Kay, little Kay, when did he come?" asked Gerda; "was he among the crowd?"

"Presently, presently; we have just come to him. On the third day arrived a youth with neither horse nor carriage; gaily he marched up to the palace; his eyes sparkled like yours; he had long beautiful hair, but was very meanly clad."

"That was Kay!" exclaimed Gerda. "Oh then I have found him," and she clapped her hands with delight.

"He carried a knapsack on his back," said the raven.

"No, not a knapsack," said Gerda, "a sledge, for he had a sledge with him when he left home."

"It is possible," rejoined the raven, "I did not look very closely, but this I heard from my beloved, that when he entered

"He carried a knapsack on his back"

the palace gates and saw the royal guard in silver, and the lackeys in gold upon the staircase, he did not seem in the least confused, but nodded pleasantly and said to them, 'It must be very tedious standing out here; I prefer going in.' The halls glistened with light, cabinet councilors and excellencies were walking about bare-footed and carrying golden keys—it was just a place to make a man solemn and silent—and the youth's boots creaked horribly, yet he was not at all afraid."

"That most certainly was Kay!" said Gerda; "I know he had new boots; I have heard them creak in my grandmother's room."

"Indeed they did creak," said the raven, "but merrily went he up to the princess, who was sitting upon a pearl as large as a spinning-wheel, whilst all the ladies of the court, with the maids of honor and their handmaidens, ranged in order, stood on one side, and all the gentlemen in waiting, with their gentlemen, and their gentlemen's gentlemen, who also kept pages, stood ranged in order on the other side, and the nearer they were to the door the prouder they looked. The gentlemen's page, who always wears slippers, one dare hardly look at, so proudly he stands at the door."

"That must be dreadful!" said little Gerda. "And has Kay really won the princess?"

"Had I not been a raven I should have won her myself, notwithstanding my being betrothed. The young man spoke as well as I speak when I converse in Ravenish; that I have heard from my tame beloved. He was handsome and lively—'He did not come to woo her,' he said, 'he had only come to hear the wisdom of the princess,' and he liked her much, and she liked him in return."

And the nearer they were to the door the prouder they looked

"Yes, to be sure, that was Kay," said Gerda; "he was so clever, he could reckon in his head, even fractions! Oh, will you not take me into the palace?"

"Ah! that is easily said," replied the raven, "but how is it to be done? I will talk it over with my tame beloved; she will advise us what to do, for I must tell you that such a little girl as you are will never gain permission to enter publicly."

"Yes, I shall!" cried Gerda. "When Kay knows that I am here, he will immediately come out and fetch me."

"Wait for me at the trellis yonder," said the raven. He wagged his head and away he flew.

The raven did not return till late in the evening. "Caw, caw," said he. "My tame beloved greets you kindly, and sends you a piece of bread which she took from the kitchen; there is plenty of bread there, and you must certainly be hungry. It is not possible for you to enter the palace, for you have bare feet; the royal guard in silver uniform, and the lackeys in gold, would never permit it; but do not weep, thou shalt go there. My beloved knows a little back staircase leading to the sleeping apartments, and she knows also where to find the key."

And they went into the garden, down the grand avenue, where the leaves dropped upon them as they passed along, and, when the lights in the palace one by one had all been extinguished, the raven took Gerda to a back-door which stood half open. Oh, how Gerda's heart beat with fear and expectation! It was just as though she was about to do something wrong, although she only wanted to know whether Kay was really there—yes, it must be he, she remembered so well his bright eyes and long hair. She would see if his smile were the same as it used to be when they

PLATE 7.
"He did not come to woo her," he said, "he had only
come to hear the wisdom of the princess"

The raven

sat together under the rose-trees. He would be so glad to see her, to hear how far she had come for his sake, how all his home mourned his absence. Her heart trembled with fear and joy.

They went up the staircase. A small lamp placed on a cabinet gave a glimmering light; on the floor stood the tame raven, who first turned her head on all sides, and then looked at Gerda, who made her curtsy, as her grandmother had taught her.

"My betrothed has told me much about you, my good young maiden," said the tame raven; "your adventures, too, are extremely interesting! If you will take the lamp, I will show you the way. We are going straight on, we shall not meet any one now."

"It seems to me as if some one were behind us," said Gerda; and in fact there was a rushing sound as of something passing; strange-looking shadows flitted rapidly along the wall, horses with long, slender legs and fluttering manes, huntsmen, knights, and ladies.

"These are only dreams!" said the raven; "they come to amuse the great personages here at night; you will have a better opportunity of looking at them when you are in bed. I hope that when you arrive at honors and dignities you will show a grateful heart."

"Do not talk of that!" said the wood-raven.

They now entered the first saloon; its walls were covered with rose-colored satin, embroidered with gold flowers. The Dreams rustled past them, but with such rapidity that Gerda could not see them. The apartments through which they passed vied with each other in splendor, and at last they reached the sleeping-hall. In the center of this room stood a pillar of gold resembling the stem of a large palm-tree, whose leaves of glass, costly glass, formed the ceiling, and depending from the tree, hung near the door, on thick golden st alks, two beds in the form of lilies—the one was white, wherein reposed the princess, the other was red, and here must Gerda seek her playfellow, Kay. She bent aside one of the red leaves and saw a brown neck. Oh, it must be Kay! She called him by his name aloud, held the lamp close to him, the Dreams again rushed by—he awoke, turned his head, and behold! it was not Kay.

The prince resembled him only about the throat; he was, however, young and handsome; and the princess looked out from the white lily petals, and asked what was the matter. Then little Gerda wept and told her whole story, and what the ravens had done for her. "Poor child!" said the prince and princess; and they praised the ravens, and said they were not at all angry with them. Such liberties must never be taken again in their palace, but this time they should be rewarded.

"Would you like to fly away free to the woods?" asked the princess, addressing the ravens, "or to have the appointment secured to you as Court-Ravens with the perquisites belonging to the kitchen, such as crumbs and leavings?"

And both the ravens bowed low and chose the appointment at Court, for they thought of old age, and said it would be so comfortable to be well provided for in their declining years. Then the prince arose and made Gerda sleep in his bed; and she folded her little hands, thinking, "How kind both men and animals are to me!" She closed her eyes and slept soundly and sweetly, and all the Dreams flitted about her; they looked like angels from heaven, and seemed to be drawing a sledge whereon Kay sat and nodded to her. But this was only fancy, for as soon as she awoke all the beautiful visions had vanished.

The next day she was dressed from head to foot in silk and velvet. She was invited to stay at the palace and enjoy all sorts of diversions, but she begged only for a little carriage and a horse, and a pair of little boots,—all she desired was to go again into the wide world to seek Kay.

And they gave her the boots and a muff besides; she was dressed so prettily. And as soon as she was ready there drove up to the door a new carriage of pure gold with the arms of the prince and princess glittering upon it like a star, the coachman, the footman, and outriders, all wearing gold crowns. The prince and princess themselves helped her into the carriage and wished her success. The wood-raven, who was now married, accompanied her the first three miles; he sat by her side, for riding backwards was a thing he could not bear. The other raven stood at the door flapping her wings; she did not go with them on account of a headache she had felt ever since she had received her appointment, in consequence of eating too much. The carriage was well provided with sugar-plums, fruit, and gingerbread nuts.

"Farewell! farewell!" cried the prince and princess. Little Gerda wept, and the raven wept out of sympathy. But his farewell was a far sorer trial; he flew up to the branch of a tree and flapped his black wings at the carriage till it was out of sight.

And flapped his black wings at the carriage till it was out of sight

PART THE FIFTH

THE LITTLE ROBBER MAIDEN

They drove through the dark, dark forest; the carriage shone like a torch. Unfortunately its brightness attracted the eyes of the robbers who dwelt in the forest-shades; they could not bear it.

"That is gold! gold!" cried they. Forward they rushed, seized the horses, stabbed the outriders, coachman, and footmen to death, and dragged little Gerda out of the carriage.

"She is plump, she is pretty, she has been fed on nut-kernels," said the old robber-wife, who had a long, bristly beard, and eyebrows hanging like bushes over her eyes. "She is like a little fat lamb, and how smartly she is dressed!" and she drew out her bright dagger, glittering most terribly.

"Oh, oh!" cried the woman, for at the very moment she had lifted her dagger to stab Gerda, her own wild and wilful daughter jumped upon her back and bit her ear violently. "You naughty child!" said the mother.

"She shall play with me," said the little robber-maiden, "she shall give me her muff and her pretty frock, and sleep with me in my bed!" And then she bit her mother again, till the robber-wife sprang up and shrieked with pain, whilst the robbers all laughed, saying, "Look at her playing with her young one!"

"I will get into the carriage," and so spoiled and wayward was the little robber-maiden that she always had her own way, and she and Gerda sat together in the carriage, and drove over stock and stone farther and farther into the wood. The little robber-maiden was about as tall as Gerda, but much stronger; she had broad shoulders, and a very dark skin; her eyes were quite black, and had an expression almost melancholy. She put her arm round Gerda's waist, and said, "She shall not kill thee so long as I love thee! Art thou not a princess?"

"No!" said Gerda; and then she told her all that had happened to her, and how much she loved little Kay.

The robber-maiden looked earnestly in her face, shook her head, and said, "She shall not kill thee even if I do quarrel with thee; then, indeed, I would rather do it myself!" And she dried Gerda's tears, and put both her hands into the pretty muff that was so soft and warm.

The carriage at last stopped in the middle of the courtyard of the robbers' castle. This castle was half-ruined; crows and ravens flew out of the openings, and some fearfully large bull-dogs, looking as if they could devour a man in a moment, jumped round the carriage; they did not bark, for that was forbidden.

The maidens entered a large, smoky hall, where a tremendous fire was blazing on the stone floor; the smoke rose up to the ceiling, seeking a way of escape, for there was no chimney; a large caldron full of soup was boiling over the fire, whilst hares and rabbits were roasting on the spit.

"Thou shalt sleep with me and my little pets to-night!" said the robber-maiden. Then they had some food, and afterwards went to the corner wherein lay straw and a piece of carpet. Nearly a hundred pigeons were perched on staves and laths around them; they seemed to be asleep, but were startled when the little maidens approached.

"These all belong to me," said Gerda's companion, and seizing hold of one of the nearest, she held the poor bird by the feet and swung it. "Kiss it," said she, flapping it into Gerda's face. "The rabble from the wood sit up there," continued she, pointing to a number of laths fastened across a hole in the wall; "those are wood-pigeons, they would fly away if I did not keep them shut up. And here is my old favorite!" She pulled forward by the horn a reindeer who wore a bright copper ring round his neck, by which he was fastened to a large stone. "We are obliged to chain him up, or he would run away from us; every evening I tickle his neck with my sharp dagger; it makes him fear me so much!" and the robber-maiden drew out a long dagger from a gap in the wall, and passed it over the reindeer's throat; the poor animal struggled and kicked, but the girl laughed, and then she pulled Gerda into bed with her.

"Will you keep the dagger in your hand whilst you sleep?" asked Gerda, looking timidly at the dangerous plaything.

"I always sleep with my dagger by my side," replied the little robber-maiden; "one never knows what may happen. But now tell me all over again what you told me before about Kay, and the reason of your coming into the wide world all by yourself."

And Gerda again related her history, and the wood-pigeons imprisoned above listened, but the others were fast asleep. The little robber-maiden threw one arm round Gerda's neck, and holding the dagger with the other, was also soon asleep; one could hear her heavy breathing, but Gerda could not close her eyes throughout the night—she knew not what would become of her, whether she would even be suffered to live. The robbers sat round the fire drinking and singing. Oh, it was a dreadful night for the poor little girl!

Then spoke the wood-pigeons, "Coo, coo, coo! we have seen little Kay. A white fowl carried his sledge, he himself was in the

Snow Queen's chariot, which passed through the wood whilst we sat in our nest. She breathed upon us young ones as she passed, and all died of her breath excepting us two,—coo, coo, coo!"

"What are you saying?" cried Gerda; "where was the Snow Queen going? Do you know anything about it?"

"She travels most likely to Lapland, where ice and snow abide all the year round. Ask the reindeer bound to the rope there."

"Yes, ice and snow are there all through the year; it is a glorious land!" said the reindeer. "There, free and happy, one can roam through the wide sparkling valleys! There the Snow Queen has her summer-tent; her strong castle is very far off, near the North Pole, on the island called Spitsbergen."

"O Kay, dear Kay!" sighed Gerda.

"You must lie still," said the robber-maiden, "or I will thrust my dagger into your side."

When morning came Gerda repeated to her what the wood-pigeons had said, and the little robber-maiden looked grave for a moment, then nodded her head, saying, "No matter! no matter! Do you know where Lapland is?" asked she of the reindeer.

"Who should know but I?" returned the animal, his eyes kindling. "There was I born and bred, there how often have I bounded over the wild icy plains!"

"Listen to me!" said the robber-maiden to Gerda. "You see all our men are gone; my mother is still here and will remain, but towards noon she will drink a little out of the great flask, and after that she will sleep—then I will do something for you!" And so saying she jumped out of bed, sprang upon her mother, pulled her by the beard, and said, "My own dear mam, good morning!"

and the mother caressed her so roughly that she was red and blue all over; however, it was from pure love.

When her mother was fast asleep, the robber-maiden went up to the reindeer, and said, "I should have great pleasure in stroking you a few more times with my sharp dagger, for then you look so droll, but never mind, I will unloose your chain and help you to escape, on condition that you run as fast as you can to Lapland, and take this little girl to the castle of the Snow Queen, where her playfellow is. You must have heard her story, for she speaks loud enough, and you know well how to listen."

The reindeer bounded with joy, and the robber-maiden lifted Gerda on his back, taking the precaution to bind her on firmly, as well as to give her a little cushion to sit on. "And here," said she, "are your fur boots, you will need them in that cold country; the muff I must keep myself, it is too pretty to part with; but you shall not be frozen. Here are my mother's huge gloves, they reach up to the elbow; put them on now—your hands look as clumsy as my old mother's!"

And Gerda shed tears of joy.

"I cannot bear to see you crying!" said the little robber maiden, "you ought to look glad; see, here are two loaves and a piece of bacon for you, that you may not be hungry on the way." She fastened this provender also on the reindeer's back, opened the door, called away the great dogs, and then cutting asunder with her dagger the rope which bound the reindeer, shouted to him, "Now then, run! but take good care of the little girl."

And Gerda stretched out her hands to the robber-maiden and bade her farewell, and the reindeer fleeted through the forest, over stock and stone, over desert and heath, over meadow and moor. The wolves howled and the ravens shrieked. "Isch! Isch!" a red light flashed—one might have fancied the sky was sneezing.

"Those are my dear old Northern Lights!" said the reindeer; "look at them, how beautiful they are!" And he ran faster than ever, night and day he ran—the loaves were eaten, so was the bacon—at last they were in Lapland.

PART THE SIXTH

THE LAPLAND WOMAN AND THE FINLAND WOMAN

They stopped at a little hut, a wretched hut it was; the roof very nearly touched the ground, and the door was so low that whoever wished to go either in or out was obliged to crawl upon hands and knees. No one was at home except the old Lapland woman, who was busy boiling fish over a lamp filled with train oil. The reindeer related to her Gerda's whole history, not, however, till after he had made her acquainted with his own, which appeared to him of much more importance. Poor Gerda, meanwhile, was so overpowered by the cold that she could not speak.

"Ah, poor things!" said the Lapland woman, "you have still a long way before you! You have a hundred miles to run before you can arrive in Finland: the Snow Queen dwells there, and burns blue lights every evening. I will write for you a few words on a piece of dried stock-fish—paper I have none—and you may take it with you to the wise Finland woman who lives there; she will advise you better than I can."

So when Gerda had well warmed herself and taken some food, the Lapland woman wrote a few words on a dried stock-fish, bade Gerda take care of it, and bound her once more firmly on the reindeer's back.

Onwards they sped, the wondrous Northern Lights, now of the loveliest, brightest blue color, shone all through the night, and amidst these splendid illuminations they arrived in Finland, and knocked at the chimney of the wise-woman, for door to her house she had none.

Hot, very hot was it within—so much so that the wise woman wore scarcely any clothing; she was low in stature and very dirty. She immediately loosened little Gerda's dress, took off her fur boots and thick gloves, laid a piece of ice on the reindeer's head, and then read what was written on the stock-fish. She read it three times. After the third reading she knew it by heart, and threw the fish into the porridge-pot, for it might make a very excellent supper, and she never wasted anything.

The reindeer then repeated his own story, and when that was finished he told of little Gerda's adventures, and the wise woman twinkled her wise eyes, but spoke not a word.

"Thou art so powerful," continued the reindeer, "that I know thou canst twist all the winds of the world into a thread, of which if the pilot loosen one knot he will have a favorable wind; if he loosen the second it will blow sharp, and if he loosen the third, so tremendous a storm will arise that the trees of the forest will be uprooted, and the ship wrecked. Wilt thou not mix for this little maiden that wonderful draught which will give her the strength of twelve men, and thus enable her to overcome the Snow Queen?"

"The strength of twelve men!" repeated the wise-woman, "that would be of much use to be sure!" and she walked away, drew forth a large parchment roll from a shelf and began to read. What strange characters were seen inscribed on the scroll as the wise-woman slowly unrolled it! She read so intently that the perspiration ran down her forehead.

But the reindeer pleaded so earnestly for little Gerda, and Gerda's eyes were raised so entreatingly and tearfully, that at last the wise-woman's eyes began to twinkle again out of sympathy, and she drew the reindeer into a corner, and putting a fresh piece of ice upon his head, whispered thus:

"Little Kay is still with the Snow Queen, in whose abode everything is according to his taste, and therefore he believes it to be the best place in the world. But that is because he has a glass splinter in his heart, and a glass splinter in his eye—until he has got rid of them he will never feel like a human being, and the Snow Queen will always maintain her influence over him."

"But canst thou not give something to little Gerda whereby she may overcome all these evil influences?"

"I can give her no power so great as that which she already possesses. Seest thou not how strong she is? Seest thou not that both men and animals must serve her—a poor little girl wandering barefoot through the world? Her power is greater than ours; it proceeds from her heart, from her being a loving and innocent child. If this power which she already possesses cannot give her access to the Snow Queen's palace, and enable her to free Kay's eye and heart from the glass fragment, we can do nothing for her! Two miles hence is the Snow Queen's garden; thither thou canst carry the little maiden. Put her down close by the bush bearing red berries and half covered with snow: lose no time, and hasten back to this place!"

And the wise-woman lifted Gerda on the reindeer's back, and away they went.

"Oh, I have left my boots behind! I have left my gloves behind," cried little Gerda, when it was too late. The cold was piercing, but the reindeer dared not stop; on he ran until he reached the bush with the red berries. Here he set Gerda down, kissed her, the tears rolling down his cheeks the while, and ran fast back again—which was the best thing he could do. And there stood poor Gerda, without shoes, without gloves, alone in that barren region, that terribly icy-cold Finland.

She ran on as fast as she could; a whole regiment of snow-flakes came to meet her. They did not fall from the sky, which was cloudless and bright with the Northern Lights; they ran straight along the ground, and the farther Gerda advanced the larger they grew. Gerda then remembered how large and curious the snow-flakes had appeared to her when one day she had looked at them through a burning-glass; these, however, were very much larger, they were living forms, they were in fact the Snow Queen's guards. Their shapes were the strangest that could be imagined; some looked like great ugly porcupines, others like snakes rolled into knots with their heads peering forth, and others like little fat bears with bristling hair—all, however, were alike dazzlingly white—all were living snow-flakes. Little Gerda began to repeat "Our Father": meanwhile, the cold was so intense that she could see her own breath, which, as it escaped her mouth, ascended into the air like vapor; the cold grew intense, the vapor more dense, and at length took the forms of little bright angels which, as they touched the earth, became larger and more distinct. They wore helmets on their heads, and carried shields and spears in their hands; their number increased so rapidly that, by the time Gerda had finished her prayer, a whole legion stood around her. They thrust with their spears against the horrible snow-flakes, which fell into thousands of pieces, and little Gerda walked on unhurt and undaunted. The angels touched her hands and feet, and then she scarcely felt the cold, and boldly approached the Snow Queen's palace.

But before we accompany her there, let us see what Kay is doing. He is certainly not thinking of little Gerda; least of all can he imagine that she is now standing at the palace gate.

She ran on as fast as she could

✦ PART THE SEVENTH ✦

WHICH TREATS OF THE SNOW QUEEN'S PALACE AND
OF WHAT CAME TO PASS THEREIN

The walls of the palace were formed of the driven snow, its doors and windows of the cutting winds. There were above a hundred halls, the largest of them many miles in extent, all illuminated by the Northern Lights, all alike vast, empty, icily cold, and dazzlingly white. No sounds of mirth ever resounded through these dreary spaces; no cheerful scene refreshed the sight—not even so much as a bear's ball, such as one might imagine sometimes takes place, the tempest forming a band of musicians, and the polar bears standing on their hind paws and exhibiting themselves in the oddest positions. Nor was there ever a card-assembly, wherein the cards might be held in the mouth and dealt out by paws; nor even a small select coffee-party for the white young lady foxes. Vast, empty, and cold were the Snow Queen's chambers, and the Northern Lights flashed, now high, now low, in regular gradations. In the midst of the empty, interminable snow saloon lay a frozen lake; it was broken into a thousand pieces, but these pieces so exactly resembled each other, that the breaking of them might well be deemed a work of more than human skill. The Snow Queen, when at home, always sat in the center of this lake; she used to say that she was then sitting on the Mirror of Reason, and that hers was the best, indeed the only one, in the world.

Little Kay was quite blue, nay, almost black with cold, but he did not observe it, for the Snow Queen had kissed away the shrinking feeling he used to experience, and his heart was like a lump of ice. He was busied among the sharp icy fragments, laying

The Snow Queen

and joining them together in every possible way, just as people do with what are called Chinese puzzles. Kay could form the most curious and complete figures—this was the ice-puzzle of reason—and in his eyes these figures were of the utmost importance. He often formed whole words, but there was one word he could never succeed in forming—it was Eternity. The Snow Queen had said to him, "When thou canst put that figure together, thou shalt become thine own master and I will give thee the whole world, and a new pair of skates besides."

But he could never do it.

"Now I am going to the warm countries," said the Snow Queen. "I shall flit through the air, and look into the black caldrons"—she meant the burning mountains, Etna and Vesuvius. "I shall whiten them a little; that will be good for the citrons and vineyards." So away flew the Snow Queen, leaving Kay sitting all alone in the large empty hall of ice. He looked at the fragments, and thought and thought till his head ached. He sat so still and so stiff that one might have fancied that he too was frozen.

Cold and cutting blew the winds when little Gerda passed through the palace gates, but she repeated her evening prayer, and they immediately sank to rest. She entered the large, cold, empty hall: she saw Kay, she recognized him, she flew upon his neck, she held him fast, and cried, "Kay! dear, dear Kay! I have found thee at last!"

But he sat still as before, cold, silent, motionless; his unkindness wounded poor Gerda deeply. Hot and bitter were the tears she shed; they fell upon his breast, they reached his heart, they thawed the ice and dissolved the tiny splinter of glass within it. He looked at her whilst she sang her hymn—

> "Our roses bloom and fade away,
> Our Infant Lord abides alway;
> May we be blessed His face to see,
> And ever little children be!"

Then Kay burst into tears. He wept till the glass splinter floated in his eye and fell with his tears; he knew his old companion immediately, and exclaimed with joy, "Gerda, my dear little Gerda, where hast thou been all this time?—and where have I been?"

He looked around him. "How cold it is here! how wide and empty!" and he embraced Gerda, whilst she laughed and wept by

She entered the large, cold, empty hall

turns. Even the pieces of ice took part in their joy; they danced about merrily, and when they were wearied and lay down they formed of their own accord the mystical letters of which the Snow Queen had said that when Kay could put them together he should be his own master, and that she would give him the whole world, with a new pair of skates besides.

And Gerda kissed his cheeks, whereupon they became fresh and glowing as ever; she kissed his eyes, and they sparkled like her own; she kissed his hands and feet, and he was once more healthy and merry. The Snow Queen might now come home as soon as she liked—it mattered not; Kay's charter of freedom stood written on the mirror in bright icy characters.

They took each other by the hand, and wandered forth out of the palace, talking meanwhile about the aged grandmother and the rose-trees on the roof of their houses; and as they walked on, the winds were hushed into a calm, and the sun burst forth in splendor from among the dark storm-clouds. When they arrived at the bush with the red berries, they found the reindeer standing by awaiting their arrival; he had brought with him another and younger reindeer, whose udders were full, and who gladly gave her warm milk to refresh the young travellers.

The old reindeer and the young hind now carried Kay and Gerda on their backs, first to the little hot room of the wise-woman of Finland, where they warmed themselves, and received advice how to proceed in their journey home, and afterwards to the abode of the Lapland woman, who made them some new clothes and provided them with a sledge.

The whole party now ran on together till they came to the boundary of the country; but just where the green leaves began to sprout, the Lapland woman and the two reindeers took their leave. "Farewell! farewell!" said they all. And the first little birds they had seen for many a long day began to chirp, and warble their pretty songs; and the trees of the forest burst upon them full of rich and variously tinted foliage. Suddenly the green boughs parted asunder, and a spirited horse galloped up. Gerda knew it well, for it was the one which had been harnessed to her gold coach; and on it sat a young girl wearing a bright scarlet cap, and with pistols on the holster before her. It was indeed no other than the robber-maiden, who, weary of her home in the forest, was going on her travels, first to the north and afterwards to other parts of

The little robber-maiden

the world. She at once recognized Gerda, and Gerda had not forgotten her. Most joyful was their greeting.

"A fine gentleman you are, to be sure, you graceless young truant!" said she to Kay. "I should like to know if you deserved that any one should be running to the end of the world on your account!"

But Gerda stroked her cheeks, and asked after the prince and princess.

"They are gone travelling into foreign countries," replied the robber-maiden.

"And the raven?" asked Gerda.

"Ah! the raven is dead," returned she. "The tame beloved has become a widow; so she hops about with a piece of worsted wound round her leg; she moans most piteously, and chatters more than ever! But tell me now all that has happened to you, and how you managed to pick up your old playfellow."

And Gerda and Kay told their story.

"Snip-snap-snurre-basselurre!" said the robber-maiden. She pressed the hands of both, promised that if ever she passed through their town she would pay them a visit, and then bade them farewell, and rode away out into the wide world.

Kay and Gerda walked on hand in hand, and wherever they went it was spring, beautiful spring, with its bright flowers and green leaves.

They arrived at a large town, the church bells were ringing merrily, and they immediately recognized the high towers rising into the sky—it was the town wherein they had lived. Joyfully they passed through the streets, joyfully they stopped at the door of Gerda's grandmother. They walked up the stairs and entered the well-known room. The clock said "Tick, tick!" and the hands moved as before. Only one alteration could they find, and that was in themselves, for they saw that they were now full-grown persons. The rose-trees on the roof blossomed in front of the open window, and there beneath them stood the children's stools. Kay and Gerda went and sat down upon them, still holding each other by the hands; the cold, hollow splendor of the Snow Queen's palace they had forgotten, it seemed to them only an unpleasant dream. The grandmother meanwhile sat amid God's bright sunshine, and read from the Bible these words: "Unless ye become as little children, ye shall not enter into the kingdom of heaven."

And Kay and Gerda gazed on each other; they now understood the words of their hymn—

> "Our roses bloom and fade away,
>   Our Infant Lord abides alway;
>   May we be blessed His face to see,
>   And ever little children be!"

There they sat, those two happy ones, grown-up and yet children—children in heart, while all around them glowed bright summer,—warm, glorious summer.

The Elfin-King's housekeeper

Elfin-Mount

SEVERAL LARGE LIZARDS WERE RUNNING NIMBLY IN AND OUT among the clefts of an old tree; they could understand each other perfectly well, for they all spoke the lizards' language. "Only hear what a rumbling and grumbling there is in the old Elfin-mount yonder!" observed one lizard. "I have not been able to close my eyes for the last two nights; I might as well have had the toothache, for the sleep I have had!"

"There is something in the wind, most certainly!" rejoined the second lizard. "They raise the Mount upon four red pillars till cock-crowing; there is a regular cleaning and dusting going on, and the Elfin-maidens are learning new dances—such a stamping they make in them! There is certainly something in the wind!"

"Yes; I have been talking it over with an earth-worm of my acquaintance," said a third lizard. "The earth-worm has just come from the Mount; he has been grubbing in the ground there for days and nights together, and has overheard a good deal; he can't see at all, poor wretch! but no one can be quicker than he is at feeling and hearing. They are expecting strangers at the Elfin-mount—distinguished strangers; but who they are, the earth-worm would not say; most likely he did not know. All the wills-o'-the-wisp are engaged to form a procession of torches—so they call it; and all the silver and gold, of which there is such a store in the Elfin-mount, is being fresh rubbed up, and set out to shine in the moonlight."

"But who can these strangers be?" exclaimed all the lizards with one voice. "What can be in the wind? Only listen!—what buzzing and humming!"

Just then the Elfin-mount parted asunder; and an elderly Elfin damsel came tripping out—she was the old Elfin-King's housekeeper, and distantly related to his family, on which account she wore an amber heart on her forehead, but was otherwise plainly dressed. Like all other elves, she was hollow in the back. She was very quick and light-footed; trip—trip—trip, away she ran, straight into the marsh, to the night raven. "You are invited to Elfin-mount, for this very evening," said she; "but will you not first do us a very great kindness, and be the bearer of the other invitations? You do not keep house, yourself, you know; so you can easily oblige us. We are expecting some very distinguished strangers, Trolds in fact; and his Elfin Majesty intends to welcome them in person."

"Who are to be invited?" inquired the night-raven.

Why, to the grand ball all the world may come; even men, if they could but talk in their sleep, or do a little bit of anything in our way. But the first banquet must be very select; none but guests of the very highest rank must be present. To say the truth, I and the King have been having a little dispute; for I insist, that not even ghosts may be admitted to-night. The Mer-King and his daughters must be invited first; they don't much like coming on land, but I'll promise they shall each have a wet stone, or, perhaps, something better still, to sit on; and then, I think, they cannot possibly refuse us this time. All old Trolds of the first rank we must have; also, the River-Spirit and the Nisses; and, I fancy, we cannot pass over the Death-Horse and Kirkegrim; true, they do not belong to our set, they are too solemn for us, but they are connected with the family, and pay us regular visits."

The Mer-King must be invited first

"Caw!" said the night-raven; and away he flew to bear the invitations.

The Elfin-maidens were still dancing in the Elfin-mount; they danced with long scarfs woven from mist and moonlight, and for those who like that sort of thing it looks pretty enough. The large state-room in the Mount had been regularly cleaned and cleared out; the floor had been washed with moonshine, and the walls rubbed with witches' fat till they shone as tulips do when held up to the light. In the kitchen, frogs were roasting on the spit; while divers other choice dishes, such as mushroom seed, hemlock soup, etc., were prepared or preparing. These were to supply the first courses; rusty nails, bits of colored glass, and such like dainties, were to come in for the dessert; there was also bright saltpeter wine, and ale brewed in the brewery of the Wise Witch of the Moor.

The old Elfin-King's gold crown had been fresh rubbed with powdered slate-pencil; new curtains had been hung up in all the sleeping-rooms,—yes, there was indeed a rare bustle and commotion.

"Now, we must have the rooms scented with cows' hairs and swine's bristles; and then, I think, I shall have done my part!" said the Elfin-King's housekeeper.

"Dear papa," said the youngest of the daughters, "won't you tell me now who these grand visitors are?"

"Well!" replied His Majesty, "I suppose there's no use in keeping it a secret. Let two of my daughters get themselves ready for their wedding-day, that's all! Two of them most certainly will be married. The Chief of the Norwegian Trolds, he who dwells in old Dofrefield, and has so many castles of freestone among these rocky fastnesses, besides a gold-mine,—which is a capital thing, let me tell you,—he is coming down here with his two boys, who are both to choose themselves a bride. Such an honest, straightforward, true old Norseman is this mountain chief! so merry and jovial! he and I are old comrades; he came down here years ago to fetch his wife; she is dead now; she was the daughter of the Rock-King at Möen. Oh, how I long to see the old Norseman again! His sons, they say, are rough unmannerly cubs, but perhaps report may have done them injustice, and at any rate they are sure to improve in a year or two, when they have sown their wild oats. Let me see how you will polish them up!"

"And how soon are they to be here?" inquired his youngest daughter again.

"That depends on wind and weather!" returned the Elfin-King. "They travel economically; they come at the ship's convenience. I wanted them to pass over by Sweden, but the old man would not hear of that. He does not keep pace with the times, that's the only fault I can find with him."

Just then two wills-o'-the-wisp were seen dancing up in a vast hurry, each trying to get before the other, and to be the first to bring the news.

"They come, they come!" cried both with one voice.

"Give me my crown, and let me stand in the moonlight!" said the Elfin-King.

And his seven daughters lifted their long scarfs and bowed low to the earth.

There stood the Trold Chief from the Dofrefield, wearing a crown composed of icicles and polished pine cones; for the rest, he was equipped in a bear-skin cloak and sledge-boots; his sons were clad more slightly, and kept their throats uncovered, by way of showing that they cared nothing about the cold.

"Is that a mount?" asked the youngest of them, pointing to it. "Why, up in Norway we should call it a cave!"

"You foolish boy!" replied his father; "a cave you go into, a mount you go up! Where are your eyes, not to see the difference?"

The only thing that surprised them in this country, they said, was that the people should speak and understand their language.

"Behave yourselves now!" said the old man; "don't let your host fancy you never went into decent company before!"

And now they all entered the Elfin-mount, into the grand saloon, where a really very select party was assembled, although at such short notice that it seemed almost as though some fortunate gust of wind had blown them together. And every possible arrangement had been made for the comfort of each of the guests; the Mer-King's family, for instance, sat at table in large tubs of water, and they declared they felt quite as if they were at home. All behaved with strict good-breeding except the two young northern Trolds, who at last so far forgot themselves as to put their legs on the table.

"Take your legs away from the plates!" said their father, and they obeyed, but not so readily as they might have done. Presently they took some pine cones out of their pockets and began pelting the lady who sat between them, and then, finding their boots incommode them, they took them off, and coolly gave them to this lady to hold. But their father, the old mountain Chief, conducted himself very differently; he talked so delightfully about the proud Norse mountains, and the torrents, white with dancing spray, that dashed foaming down their rocky steeps with a noise loud and hoarse as thunder, yet musical as the full burst of an organ, touched by a master hand; he told of the salmon leaping up from the wild waters while the Neck was playing on his golden harp; he told of the star-light winter nights when the sledge bells tinkled so merrily, and the youths ran with lighted torches over the icy crust, so glassy and transparent that through it they could see the fishes whirling to and fro in deadly terror beneath their feet; he told of the gallant northern youths and pretty maidens singing songs of old time, and dancing the Hallinge dance,—yes, so charmingly he described all this, that you could not but fancy you heard and saw it all. Oh fie, for shame: all of a sudden the mountain Chief turned round upon the elderly Elfin maiden, and gave her a cousinly salute, and he was not yet connected ever so remotely with the family.

The young Elfin-maidens were now called upon to dance. First they danced simple dances, then stamping dances, and they did both remarkably well. Last came the most difficult of all, the "Dance out of the dance," as it was called. Bravo! how long their legs seemed to grow, and how they whirled and spun about! You could hardly distinguish legs from arms, or arms from legs. Round and round they went, such whirling and twirling, such whirring and whizzing there was that it made the death-horse feel quite dizzy, and at last he grew so unwell that he was obliged to leave the table.

"Hurrah!" cried the mountain Chief, "they know how to use their limbs with a vengeance! but can they do nothing else than dance, stretch out their feet, and spin round like a whirlwind?"

"You shall judge for yourself," replied the Elfin-King, and here he called the eldest of his daughters to him. She was transparent and fair as moonlight; she was, in fact, the most delicate of all the sisters; she put a white wand between her lips and vanished: that was her accomplishment.

But the mountain Chief said he should not at all like his wife to possess such an accomplishment as this, and he did not think his sons would like it either.

The second could walk by the side of herself, just as though she had a shadow, which elves and trolds never have.

The accomplishment of the third sister was of quite another kind: she had learned how to brew good ale from the Wise Witch of the Moor, and she also knew how to lard alder-wood with glow-worms.

"She will make a capital housewife," remarked the old mountain Chief.

And now advanced the fourth Elfin damsel; she carried a large gold harp, and no sooner had she struck the first chord than all the company lifted their left feet—for elves are left-sided—and when she struck the second chord, they were all compelled to do whatever she wished.

PLATE 8.
Round and round they went, such whirling
and twirling

"A dangerous lady, indeed!" said the old Trold Chief. Both of his sons now got up and strode out of the mount; they were heartily weary of these accomplishments.

"And what can the next daughter do?" asked the mountain Chief.

"I have learned to love the north," replied she, "and I have resolved never to marry unless I may go to Norway."

But the youngest of the sisters whispered to the old man, "That is only because she has heard an old Norse rhyme, which says that when the end of the world shall come, the Norwegian rocks shall stand firm amid the ruins; she is very much afraid of death, and therefore she wants to go to Norway."

"Ho, ho!" cried the mountain Chief, "sits the wind in that quarter? But what can the seventh and last do?"

"The sixth comes before the seventh," said the Elfin-King; for he could count better than to make such a mistake. How ever, the sixth seemed in no hurry to come forward.

"I can only tell people the truth," said she. "Let no one trouble himself about me; I have enough to do to sew my shroud!"

And now came the seventh and last, and what could she do? Why, she could tell fairy tales, as many as any one could wish to hear.

"Here are my five fingers," said the mountain Chief; "tell me a story for each finger."

And the Elfin-maiden took hold of his wrist, and told her stories, and he laughed till his sides ached, and when she came to the finger that wore a gold ring, as though it knew it might be wanted, the mountain Chief suddenly exclaimed, "Hold fast what thou hast; the hand is thine! I will have thee myself to wife!" But the Elfin-maiden said that she had still two more stories to tell, one for the ring-finger, and another for the little finger.

"Keep them for next winter, we'll hear them then," replied the mountain Chief. "And we'll hear about the 'Loves of the Fir-Tree and the Birch,' about the Valkyria's gifts too, for we all love fairy legends in Norway, and no one there can tell them so charmingly as thou dost. And then we will sit in our rocky halls, whilst the fir-logs are blazing and crackling in the stove, and drink mead out of the golden horns of the old Norse kings; the Neck has taught me a few of his rare old ditties, besides the Garbo will often come and pay us a visit, and he will sing thee all the sweet songs that the mountain maidens sang in days of yore;—that will be most delightful! The salmon in the torrent will spring up and beat himself against the rock walls, but in vain, he will not be able to get in. Oh, thou canst not imagine what a happy, glorious life we lead in that dear old Norway! But where are the boys?"

"I will have thee myself
to wife"

Where were the boys? Why, they were racing about in the fields and blowing out the poor wills-o'-the-wisp, who were just ranging themselves in the proper order to make a procession of torches.

"What do you mean by making all this riot?" inquired the mountain Chief. "I have been choosing you a mother; now you come and choose yourselves wives from among your aunts."

But his sons said they would rather make speeches and drink toasts; they had not the slightest wish to marry. And accordingly they made speeches, tossed off their glasses and turned them topsy-turvy on the table, to show that they were quite empty; after this they took off their coats, and most unceremoniously lay down on the table and went to sleep. But the old mountain Chief, the while, danced round the hall with his young bride, and exchanged boots with her, because that is not so vulgar as exchanging rings.

"Listen, the cock is crowing!" exclaimed the lady-house-keeper. "We must make haste and shut the window-shutters close, or the sun will scorch our complexions."

And herewith Elfin-mount closed.

But outside, in the cloven trunk, the lizards kept running up and down, and one and all declared, "What a capital fellow that old Norwegian Trold is!" "For my part, I prefer the boys," said the earth-worm;—but he, poor wretch, could see nothing either of them or of their father, so his opinion was not worth much.

THE · MARSH · KING'S · DAUGHTER ·

THE MARSH KING'S
DAUGHTER

THE STORKS TELL THEIR YOUNG ONES EVER SO MANY FAIRY
tales, all of them from the fen and the moss. Generally the tales
are suited to the youngsters' age and understanding. The baby
birds are pleased if they are told just "kribly, krably, plurry-
murry!" which they think wonderful; but the older ones will
have something with more sense in it, or, at the least, a tale about
themselves. Of the two oldest and longest tales which have been
told among the storks, one we all know—that about Moses, who
was placed by his mother in an ark on the waters of the Nile, was
found by the king's daughter, and then was taught all learning,
and became a great man, and no one knows where he was buried.
Everybody has heard that tale.

But the other story is not known at all even now; perhaps
because it is really a chimney-corner tale. It has been handed
down by mother-stork to mother-stork for hundreds of years, and
each in turn has told it better, till now we are telling it best of all.

The first pair of storks who knew it had their summer
quarters on a Viking's log-house by the moor in Wendsyssel,
which is in the county of Hjörring, near Skagen in Jutland, if we
want to be accurate. To this day there is still an enormous great

moss there. You can read all about it in your geography book. The moss lies where was once the bottom of the sea, before the great upheaval of the land; and now it stretches for miles, surrounded on all sides by watery meadows and quivering bog, with turf-moss cloud-berries and stunted trees growing. A fog hangs over it almost continually, and till about seventy years ago wolves were still found there. It may certainly be called a wild moor, and you can imagine what lack of paths and what abundance of swamp and sea was there thousands of years ago. In that waste man saw ages back just what he sees to-day. The reeds were just as high, with the same kind of long leaves and purplish-brown, feathery flowers as they have now; the birches stood with white bark and fine, loose-hung leaves just as they now stand; and for the living creatures that came there, why, the fly wore its gauze suit of just the same cut as now, and the color of the stork's dress was white and black, with red stockings. On the other hand, the men of that time wore different clothes from those we wear. But whoever it was, poor peasant or free hunter, that trod on the quagmire, it happened thousands of years ago just as it does to-day—in he went and down he sank, down to the Marsh King, as they called him, who reigned beneath in the great Moss Kingdom.

He was called also the Mire King, but we will call him by the stork's name for him—Marsh King. People know very little about how he governed, but perhaps that is just as well.

Near to the moss, and right in the Liim Fjord, stood the Viking's log-house, with paved cellar and tower two stories high. On the roof the storks had built their nest. Mother-stork sat on her eggs, and was positive they would turn out well.

One evening father-stork had been out for a long time, and when he came home he seemed excited and flurried.

"I've dreadful news for you!" he said to mother-stork.

"Don't get excited," said she. "Remember I'm sitting on my eggs, and I might be upset by it, and then the eggs would suffer."

"You must know it!" he answered. "She has come here, our landlord's daughter in Egypt! She has ventured on the journey here, and she is lost!"

"Why, she is of fairy descent! Tell me all about it; you know I can't bear to wait at this time, when I'm sitting."

"Listen, mother. It's as you told me. She has believed what the doctor said, that the moor-flowers here could do her sick father good, and so she has flown here in a feather-dress with the other winged princesses, who have to come to the north every year to bathe and renew their youth. She has come, and she is lost!"

"You're getting too long-winded!" said mother-stork. "The eggs may be chilled! I can't bear to be excited!"

"I have watched," said father-stork, "and in the evening, when I went into the reeds, where the quagmire is able to bear me, there came three swans. Something in the way they flew told me, 'Watch; that isn't a real swan; it's only swan feathers.' You know the feeling, mother, as well as I do; you can tell if it is right."

"Yes, certainly," said she; "but tell me about the princess. I'm tired of hearing about the swan's feathers."

"Here, in the middle of the moor, you know," said father-stork, "is a kind of lake; you can see a part of it if you stand up. There, by the reeds and the green quagmire, lies a great elder-stump. The three swans lighted on it, flapped their wings, and looked round them. Then one of them threw off her swan's plumage, and I saw it was our own princess, of our house in Egypt. Then she sat down, and she had no other covering than her own long, black hair. I heard her ask the two others to take great care of her swan-skin while she plunged under the water to gather a flower which she thought she saw. They nodded, and lifted up the loose feather-dress. 'I wonder what they mean to do with it,' said I to myself; and no doubt she asked them the same. And she got an answer, something she could see for herself. They flew aloft with her feather-dress! 'Sink down,' they cried; 'you shall never fly in the swan-skin again; never see Egypt again! Stay in the moss!' And so they tore her feather-dress into a hundred pieces, till the feathers flew about as if it was snowing, and off flew the two good-for-nothing princesses."

"Oh, how dreadful!" said mother-stork. "I can't bear to hear it. But, tell me, what else happened?"

"Our princess moaned and wept. Her tears fell on the elder-stump, and it was quite moved, for it was the Marsh King himself, who lives in the quagmire. I saw the stump turn itself, so it wasn't only a trunk, for it put out long, muddy boughs like arms. Then the unhappy girl was frightened, and sprang aside into the quivering marsh, which will not bear me, much less her. In at once she sank, and down with her went the elder-stump—it was he who pulled her down. Then a few big black bubbles, and no trace of her left. She is engulfed in the marsh, and will never return to Egypt with her flower. You couldn't have borne to see it, mother!"

"You shouldn't have told me anything of the sort just now; it may affect the eggs. The princess can take good care of herself. She'll get help easily enough. Had it been you or I, there would have been an end of us."

"However, I'll go day by day to see about it," said father-stork; and so he did.

The days and months went by. He saw at last one day that right from the bottom of the marsh a green stalk pushed up till it reached the surface of the water. Out of it grew a leaf, that grew wider and wider, and close to it a bud put out. Then one morning, as the stork was flying over it, it opened, with the sun's warmth, into a full-blown flower, in the middle of which lay a beautiful child, a little girl, as if she were fresh from the bath. So like was the child to the princess from Egypt, that at first the stork believed it to be herself

It was he who pulled her down

turned a child again. But when he thought it over, he decided that it was more likely to be the child of the princess and the Marsh King, and that was why she was lying in a water lily.

"She mustn't be left lying there," thought father-stork, "and there are too many already in my nest. But I have it! The Viking's wife has no children, and she has often wished for a little one.

Yes, I get the name for bringing the babies; I will do it in sober truth for once! I'll fly to the Viking's wife with the child. They'll be delighted!"

So the stork took the little girl, flew to the log-house, made a hole with his beak in the window, with panes made of bladder, laid the child on the bosom of the Viking's wife, and flew away to mother-stork to tell her all about it. Her young ones heard it too, for they were now old enough.

"Listen; the princess is not dead. She has sent her little one up, and the child has a home found for her."

"Yes, so I said from the first," said mother-stork. "Now think a little about your own children. It's almost time for our journey. I begin to feel a tingling under my wings. The cuckoo and the nightingale are off already, and I hear the quails chattering about it, and saying that we shall soon have a favorable wind. Our young ones are quite fit for training, I'm sure."

Glad indeed was the Viking's wife when she woke in the morning to find the beautiful little child near her side. She kissed and fondled it, but it screamed with passion, and threw out its arms and legs, and seemed utterly miserable. At last it cried itself to sleep, and there it lay, one of the prettiest babies you could set eyes on.

The Viking's wife was so happy, so gay, so well, that she could not but hope that her husband and his men would return as suddenly as the little one had come, and so she and all her household busied themselves to get everything into order. The long colored tapestries, which she and her maidens had woven with figures of their gods—Odin, Thor, Freya, as they were called—were hung up; the slaves were set to polish the old shields used for decoration; cushions were arranged on the benches, and dry wood placed on the hearth in the middle of the hall, so that the fire could be lit in a moment. The Viking's wife took her share in the work, so that by the evening she was very tired, and slept soundly.

When she woke towards daybreak she was terribly frightened. The little child had vanished! She sprang up, lighted a brand, and looked everywhere around. There, just at the foot of the bed where she had lain, was, not a baby, but a great ugly toad! In utter disgust at it she took a heavy stick to kill it, but the creature looked at her with such wonderfully sad eyes that she could not destroy it. Once more she gazed round; the toad uttered a faint, mournful croak. She started, and sprang from the bedside to the window, and opened it. At that moment the sun rose, and cast its rays upon the bed and upon the great toad. All at once it seemed that the creature's wide mouth shrank, and became small and rosy; the limbs filled out into the most charming shape. It was her own beautiful babe that lay there, not the hideous reptile!

"What is this?" cried the dame. "Was it an ill dream? Yes, there is my own sweet elfin child lying there!" She kissed it, and pressed it to her heart; but it fought and bit like a wild kitten!

The Viking, however, did not come that day, nor the next; for though he was on his way, the wind was against him as it blew to the south for the storks. Fair wind for one is foul for the other.

In those two days and nights the Viking's wife saw clearly how it was with her little child. And dreadful indeed was the spell that lay on it. By day it was as beautiful as an angel of light, but it had a bad, evil disposition. By night, on the other hand, it was a hideous toad, quiet, sad, with sorrowful eyes. It had two natures, which changed with its outward form. And so it was that the baby, brought by the stork, had by daylight its mother's own rightful shape, but its father's temper; while again, night made the kinship with him evident in the bodily form, in which, however, dwelt the mother's mind and heart. Who could loose the spell cast by the power of witchcraft? The Viking's wife was worn and distressed about it, and her heart was heavy for the unhappy being, of whose condition she did not think that she dared tell her husband if he came home then, for he would certainly follow the custom and practice of the time, and expose the poor child on the high-road for any one that liked to take away. The good dame had not the heart to do this: her husband should see the child only by daylight.

One morning the wings of storks were heard above the roof. More than a hundred pairs of the birds had rested themselves for the night after their heavy exercise, and they now flew up, preparatory to starting southwards.

"All ready, and the wives and children?" was their cry.

"Oh, I'm so light," said the young storks. "My bones feel all kribly-krably, as if I was filled with live frogs! How splendid it is to have to go abroad!"

"Keep up in the flight," said father and mother, "and don't chatter so much; it tires the chest."

And they flew.

At the same moment a horn sounded over the moor. The Viking had landed with all his men, returning laden with booty from the coasts of Gaul, where the people, like those of Britain, used to chant in their terror: "From the rage of the Northmen,

Lord, deliver us!" Guess what stir and festival now came to the Viking's stronghold near the moor! A barrel of mead was brought into hall; a huge fire was lighted; horses were slaughtered; everything went duly. The heathen priest sprinkled the slaves with warm blood, to begin their new life; the fire crackled; the smoke curled under the roof; the soot fell down from the beams—but they were used to that. Guests were invited, and received valuable gifts. Plots and treachery were forgotten; they drank deep and threw the picked bones in each other's faces in good-humored horse-play. The bard—a kind of musician, but a warrior as well, who went with them, saw their exploits, and sang about them— gave them a song in which they heard all their warrior-deeds and feats of prowess. Each verse ended with the refrain:

> "Wealth, kindred, life cannot endure,
> But the warrior's glory standeth sure."

And they all clashed upon their shields, and beat upon the table with knives and fists, and made great clamor.

The Viking's wife sat on the cross-bench in the open banqueting-hall. She wore a robe of silk, with bracelets of gold and beads of amber. She had put on her dress of state, and the bard sang of her, and told of the golden treasure she had brought to her wealthy lord, while he was delighted with the beautiful child, for he could see it by day in all its loveliness. He was well pleased with the baby's wildness, and said she would become a right warrior-maid, and fight as his champion. She did not even blink her eyes when a skillful hand cut her eyelashes with a sharp sword as a rough joke.

The barrel of mead was drained, and a second brought in, and all got well drunk, for they were folk who loved to drink their fill. They had a proverb: "The kine know when to go to stall from pasture, but the fool never knows when he has had enough." They knew it well enough, but know and do are different things. They had another proverb, too: "The dearest friend grows wearisome when he outstays his welcome." But on they stayed. Meat and mead are good: it was glorious!—and the slaves slept in the warm ashes, and dipped their fingers in the fat and licked them. Oh, it was a great time!

Once again that year the Viking went on a raid, though the autumn gales were rising. He led his men to the coast of Britain— "just over the water," he said; and his wife remained with the little girl. And truth to tell, the foster-mother soon grew fonder of the unhappy toad with the gentle eyes and deep sigh than of the beautiful child that fought and bit all about her.

The raw, dank autumn mist, "Mouthless," which devours the leaves lay over forest and moor; "Bird Featherless," as they called the snow, flew closely all around; winter was nigh at hand. The sparrows took the storks' nests for themselves, and criticized the ways of the late owners during their absence. And where were mother- and father-stork and their young ones all the time? Down in the land of Egypt, where the sun shone warm, as it does on a fine summer's day with us. Tamarinds and acacias bloomed round them; the crescent of Mahomet gleamed bright from the cupolas of the mosques; pairs and pairs of storks sat on the slender turrets, and rested after their long journey. Great flocks of them had built nest by nest on the huge pillars and broken arches of temples and forgotten cities. The date-palm raised its foliage on high, as if to keep off the glare of the sun. Grey-white pyramids stood out against the clear sky across the desert, where the ostrich raced at speed, and the lion crouched with great, wise eyes, and saw the marble sphinx that lay half-buried in the sand. The Nile flood had retired; the whole bed of the river was swarming with frogs, and to the stork family that was quite the best thing to be seen in the country. The young ones thought their eyes must be playing them tricks, it all seemed so wonderful.

"We always have it just like this in our warm country," said mother-stork; and the young ones felt their appetites grow.

"Will there be anything more to see?" said they. "Shall we go much farther into the country?"

"There is nothing better to see," said mother-stork. "At that green border is only a wild wood, where the trees crowd one upon another, and are entangled together with thorny creepers. Only an elephant with his clumsy legs can make a way there. The snakes are too large for us, and the lizards too lively. If you try to go into the desert you get your eyes full of sand in fair weather, and if there is much wind, you find yourself buried under a sand-heap. No, this is the best place. Here are frogs and locusts. I shall stop here, and you must stay with me." And they stayed.

The old ones sat in their nest on the slender minaret and rested themselves, while yet they were busy preening their feathers and rubbing their beaks on their red-stockinged legs. They would raise their necks, bow gravely, and hold up their heads with their high foreheads, fine, smooth feathers, and brown eyes glancing sharply. The young hen-storks walked gravely

The Nile flood had retired

about among the coarse reeds, stealing glances at the other young storks, and devouring a frog at every third step, or else a small snake, which they found so good for their health, and so tasty. The young males began to quarrel, beat each other with their wings, pecked, yes, stabbed till the blood flowed! And so one and another got betrothed, for that was the whole purpose of life. They built nests, and from that sprang new quarrels, for in hot countries tempers are so quick! Nevertheless, it was all delightful, especially to the old ones. Everything that one's own youngsters do becomes them. Every day there was sunshine; every day was so much taken up with eating that there was hardly time to think of amusement.

But inside the rich palace of their Egyptian landlord, as they called him, joy was unknown. Rich and mighty lord, there he lay on a couch, his limbs rigid, stretched out like a mummy, in the midst of the great hall with its many-colored walls; it looked just as if he was lying in a tulip. His kinsmen and servants stood around him; he was not dead; you could not call him alive; he existed. The healing moss-flower from the northern land, which should have been searched for and gathered by her who loved him most dearly, would never be brought. His young and beautiful daughter, who flew in swan's-plumage over sea and land, far towards the north, would never return. "She is dead and gone!" the two swan-maidens had told him on their return. They had invented a whole history of it. Said they:—

"We all three flew high in the air: a hunter saw us and shot an arrow; it struck our friend, and singing her farewell, like a dying swan, she slowly sank, in the midst of a forest lake. There we buried her, near the shore of the lake, under a fragrant weeping-birch. But we took our revenge! We bound fire under the wings of a swallow which had built under the hunter's thatched roof! The thatch caught; the house blazed up! He was burned in it, and the light shone over the lake as far as the drooping birch tree under which she is buried. She will never come back to the land of Egypt."

And so they both wept; and the father-stork, when he heard it, chattered with his beak till it rattled again.

"Lies and make-up!" said he. "I have a great mind to drive my beak into their hearts."

"And break it off!" said mother-stork. "And what good would that do? Think first of yourself and your own family; everything else is of no consequence!"

"However, I will seat myself on the edge of the open court in the morning, when all the learned doctors are met to talk about the illness. Perhaps they will come a little nearer the truth."

And the learned doctors came together, and talked and talked all about, so that the stork could not make head or tail of it—nor did anything come of it for the sickness, or for the daughter in the moor; but, nevertheless, we shall be glad to hear something about it, for we are obliged to listen to a great deal.

But now it will be a very good thing to learn what had gone before this meeting, in order to understand the story better, for at least we know as much as father-stork.

"Love brings life! The highest love supports the highest life! Only through love will he be able to secure the preservation of his life!" was what they said; and very wisely and well said it was, according to the learned.

"That's a pretty thought!" said father-stork.

"I don't rightly understand it!" said mother-stork, "and it isn't my fault, but the expressions! However, be that as it may, I've something else to think about!"

Then the learned men had spoken of love for one thing to another, of the difference there is between the affection of lovers and that of parent and child; of the love of plant and sunbeam, where the rays of the sun touch the bud and the young shoot thus comes forth—all this was expounded at such great length and in so learned a way that it was impossible for father-stork to follow it, much less to repeat it. He was quite thoughtful about it, and half closed his eyes and stood on one leg a whole day afterwards; such learning was too heavy for him to bear.

However, he understood one thing. He had heard both the common folk and those of the highest rank say the same thing from the bottom of their hearts—that it was a great misfortune for thousands of people, for the country at large, that this man should be ill and not recover; it would be a joy and blessing if he were restored to health. "But where does the flower of health grow for him?" that was what they had all inquired. They sought it from the scrolls of wisdom, from the twinkling stars, and from the winds; they had asked in all byways where they might find it, and at last the learned and wise announced, as we have said: "Love brings forth life, the life of a father," and so they said more than they themselves understood. They repeated it, and wrote it as a prescription: "Love brings forth life"; but how was the thing to be done from this prescription? There lay the difficulty. At length they came to an agreement about it; the help must come from the princess, who was attached to her father with her whole soul and heart. And then they decided how it was to be brought about (all this was more than a year and a day before): she must go by night, at the new moon, to the marble sphinx near the desert, must clear away the sand from the door with her feet, and then go through the long passage that led into the middle of one of the great pyramids, where in his mummy-case lay one of the mighty kings of old, surrounded by splendor and magnificence. Here she was to hold her ear to the lips of the dead, and then it would be revealed to her how she was to gain life and health for her father.

All this she had done, and had learned in vision that, from the deep marsh in the land of Denmark, a spot most clearly indicated, she might bring home the marsh-flower, which there in the depth of the water had touched her breast. Then he would be healed. So she flew in swan's plumage from the land of Egypt to the moor.

You see, father-stork and mother-stork were aware of all this, and now we know the story more fully than before. We remember that the Marsh King dragged her down to him; we know that for those at home she is dead and gone; only the wisest of them all said still, with mother-stork: "She takes good care of herself!" and they were obliged to wait, for that was all they knew about it.

"I believe I can steal the swans' plumage from the two good-for-nothing princesses!" said father-stork, "then they will not be able to go to the moor to work mischief. I will hide the swans' skins themselves till they are wanted."

"Where will you hide them?" asked mother-stork.

"In our nest on the moor!" said he. "I and the youngest of our brood can be helped along with them, and if they are troublesome to us, there are plenty of places on the way where we can hide them till next time of moving. One swan's dress would be enough for her, but two are better; it is well to have plenty of luggage in a northern climate!"

"You will get no thanks for it!" said mother-stork. "However, you are the master. I have nothing to say, except when I am sitting."

In the Viking's stronghold near the moor, whither the storks flew at the spring, the little girl had received her name. They had called her Helga, but that was far too sweet for such a disposition as the one possessed by this most beautiful child. Month after month it became more evident, and as years went by—whilst the storks pursued the same journey, in autumn towards the Nile, in spring towards the moor—the little child became a grown girl, and before people thought of it, she was in her sixteenth year, and the most beautiful of maidens. But the fruit was a beautiful shell, the kernel hard and rough. She was wilder than most people even in that hard gloomy age.

It was a delight to her to splash with her white hands in the hot blood of the horse which had been slaughtered as a sacrifice; in her wildness she bit off the neck of the black cock which should have been slain by the heathen priest; and she said in sober earnest to her foster-father:—

"If thine enemy came and tied a rope to the beams of the roof, and lifted it over thy chamber, whilst thou wast asleep, I should not wake thee, even if I could! I would not hear it, my blood still so hums in my ears where thou didst slap me years ago! Thou! I remember!"

But the Viking did not believe what she said; he was, like the others, infatuated with her beauty; and he did not know how disposition and appearance changed in little Helga. She would sit without a saddle, as if she had grown to the horse, when it galloped at full speed; and she would not leap off, even when it fought with other vicious horses. In all her clothes she would often cast herself from the bank into the strong current of the fjord and swim to meet the Viking when his boat was steering towards the land. She cut off the longest lock from her beautiful long hair, and made it into a string for her bow. "Self-made is well made!" she said.

The Viking's wife, according to the age and custom, was strong in will and in disposition, but towards the daughter she seemed a mild, anxious woman, for she knew that the dreadful child was bewitched.

When her mother stood on the balcony, or walked out into the courtyard, it seemed as if Helga took an evil delight in placing herself on the edge of the well, extending her arms and legs, and then leaping plump into the narrow, deep hole, where she, with her frog-nature, dived, and rose again, crawled out, just as if she was a cat, and came, dripping with water, into the lofty hall, so that the green leaves which were scattered on the floor floated about in the watery stream.

But there was one bond that restrained little Helga, and that was the dusk of the evening. Then she became quiet and pensive, and would allow herself to be called and led. She seemed to be drawn by some internal feeling to her mother, and when the sun went down and the transformation without and within her took place, she sat there quiet and melancholy, shrunken together into the figure of a toad. Her body, indeed, was now far larger than that creature's, but it was only so much the more disgusting. She looked like a miserable dwarf with frog's head, and web between the fingers. There was something of the deepest melancholy in the expression of her eyes; she had no voice but a hollow moan, just like a child that sobs in its dreams. The Viking's wife could then take her on her knees: she forgot the ugly form, and looked only at the sorrowful eyes, and more than once she said:—

"I could wish almost that thou wast always my dumb frog-child! Thou art more frightful to look at when thy beauty returns to thee."

And she wrote runes against witchcraft and disease, and cast them over the wretched girl, but she saw no change.

"Now that she is a full-grown woman, and so like the Egyptian mother," said father-stork, "one could not believe that she was once so little that she lay in a water-lily. We have never seen her mother since! She did not take care of herself, as you and the learned men thought. Year out, year in, I have flown now in all directions over the moor, but she has never made any sign. Yes, let me tell you that every year when I have come up here some days ahead of you, to mend the nest and put one thing and another straight, I have flown for a whole night, like an owl or a bat, to and fro over the open water, but it was no use! Nor have the two swan-dresses been any use which the young ones and I dragged hither from the land of the Nile. Toilsome work it was, and it took us three journeys to do it. They have now lain for many years at the bottom of the nest, and if such a disaster as a fire should happen at any time, and the log-house be burnt, they would be lost!"

"And our good nest would be lost also!" said mother-stork. "You think too little of that, and too much of the feather-dress, and your moss-princess! You had better take it to her and stay in the bog! You are a useless father to your own family; I have said that ever since I sat on an egg for the first time! I only hope that we or our young ones may not get an arrow in the wing from that mad Viking girl! She does not know what she is doing. We have lived here a little longer than she, she should remember! We never forget our obligations; we pay our taxes yearly, a feather, an egg, and a young one, as is right. Do you think, when she is outside, I feel inclined to go down there, as in the old days, and as I do in Egypt, where I am half a companion with them, without their forgetting me, and peep into tub and pot? No, I sit up here worrying myself about her—the hussy!—and about you too! You ought to have let her lie in the water-lily, and there would have been an end of her!"

"You are kinder than your words!" said father-stork. "I know you better than you know yourself."

And so he gave a jump, two heavy strokes of his wings, stretched his legs behind him, and off he flew. He sailed away, without moving his wings. At a good distance off he gave a powerful stroke; the sun shone on his white feathers; he stretched his neck and head forward! That was speed and flight!

"But he is still the handsomest of them all!" said the mother-stork, "only I don't tell him that."

Early that autumn the Viking came home with spoil and captives. Among these was a young Christian priest, one of those men who preached against the idols of the northern countries. Often at that period did the talk in the hall and in the bower of the women refer to the new faith, which had made its way into all the countries of the south, and by the holy Anskarius had been brought even to Haddeby on the Schlei. Helga herself had heard of the faith in the White Christ, who out of love to men had given Himself to save them; but for her, as they say, it had gone in at one ear and out at the other. She seemed to have only a perception of that word "love" when she crouched in that closed room in her miserable frog form. But the Viking's wife had listened to it, and felt herself wonderfully affected by the story and traditions of the Son of the only true God. The men, on coming home from their expedition, had told of the splendid temples of costly hewn stone, erected for Him whose message was love; and they brought home with them a pair of heavy golden vessels, elaborately pierced, and with a fragrant odor about them, for they were censers, which the Christian priests used to swing before the altar where no blood was ever shed, but wine and consecrated bread changed into His body and blood who had given Himself for generations yet unborn.

In the deep paved cellar of the log house the young captive Christian priest was confined, his feet and hands securely bound. The Viking's wife said that he was "as fair as Baldur," and she was touched by his distress; but young Helga wished that a rope should be drawn through his legs, and that he should be tied to the tails of wild oxen.

"Then I would set the dogs loose. Halloo! away over bog and fen, out to the moor! That would be jolly to see! jollier still to be able to follow him on his course!"

But the Viking did not choose that he should be put to death that way, but, as a denier and opposer of the high gods, he should be offered the next morning on the blood-stone in the grove—the first time that a human sacrifice had been offered there.

Young Helga asked that she might sprinkle the images of the gods and the people with his blood. She sharpened her gleaming knife, and when one of the great, ferocious dogs, of which there were a good many in the court-yard, ran across her feet, she drove the knife into its side. "That is to test it," said she; and the Viking's wife looked sadly at the wild, ill-tempered girl, and, when the night came, and the beautiful bodily form of her daughter was changed for the beauty of soul, she spoke glowing words of sorrow to her from her own afflicted spirit.

The hideous toad with the goblin's body stood before her, and fixed its brown, sorrowful eyes on her; listening and seeming to understand with the intelligence of a human being.

"Never, even to my husband, has a word fallen from my tongue about the twofold nature I endure in thee," said the Viking's wife. "There is more pity in my heart for thee than I could have believed! Great is the love of a mother; but affection never comes into thy mind! Thy heart is like the cold clod! Whence didst thou then come into my house?"

At that the hideous form trembled and shook. It seemed as if the word touched some connection between body and soul; great tears came into its eyes.

"Thy bitter trial will come some time!" said the Viking's wife; "and terrible will it be for me! Better hadst thou been abandoned on the highway as a child, and the night-frost had lulled thee into death!" And the Viking's wife wept bitter tears, and, wrathful and sad, passed behind the loose curtains which hung over the beam and divided the room.

The shrunken toad sat alone in the corner. There was silence, but after a short interval there came from her breast a half-smothered sigh. It was as if, painfully, a soul awoke to life in a corner of her heart. She took one step forward, listened, took another step, and then with her awkward hands she seized the heavy bar that was placed before the door. Gently she put it back, and quietly she drew out the peg that was stuck in over the latch. She took the lighted lamp that stood in front of the rooms; it seemed as if a strong will gave her power. She drew the iron pin out of the bolted shutter, and moved gently towards the prisoner. He was asleep. She touched him with her cold, damp hand, and when he awoke and saw that hideous form, he shuddered, as if at an evil vision. She drew her knife, severed his bonds, and made signs to him to follow her.

He called upon the holy Name, made the sign of the cross, and as the figure stood unchanged, he repeated the words of the Bible:—

"'The Lord will preserve him and keep him alive: the Lord will deliver him in time of trouble.' Who art thou? Whence is this reptile shape that yet is so full of deeds of compassion?"

The toad-figure beckoned and guided him behind sheltering curtains by a solitary way out to the stable, pointed at a horse; he mounted it, and she seated herself before him and held on by the mane of the animal. The prisoner understood her, and they rode away at a quick trot, by a path he would never have discovered, out to the open heath.

He forgot her hideous form, for the favor and mercy of the Lord were acting through this hobgoblin. He offered up pious prayers, and began to sing holy songs; and she trembled; was it the power of the prayers and hymns that acted upon her? or was it the coldness of the morning which was so quickly coming? What was it that she felt? She raised herself up in the breeze, and wished to stop the horse and spring off; but the Christian priest held her fast with all his strength, and sang aloud a Psalm, as if that would have power to loose the spell that held her in that hideous frog shape, and the horse galloped forward yet more wildly. The heaven became red; the first ray of the sun shot through the cloud, and with that clear spring of light came the change of form—she was the beautiful young girl with the demoniac, evil temper! In his arms he held a peerless maiden, and in utter terror he sprang from the horse and stopped it, for he thought he was encountering a new and deadly witchcraft. But young Helga at the same time leapt to the ground; the short child's frock reached only to her knees; she drew the sharp knife from her belt, and rushed at the startled man.

"Let me get at you!" she cried; "let me get at you, and you shall feel the knife. Yes, you are as pale as hay! Slave! Beardless boy!"

She pressed him hard; they were engaged in a severe conflict, but it was as if an unseen power gave strength to the Christian. He held her fast, and the old oak tree hard by came to his help, for its roots, half loosened from the earth, caught her feet as they slipped under them. A spring gushed forth quite close to them; he sprinkled her with the fresh water on breast and face, and charged the unclean spirit to come out of her, signing her with the cross, according to the Christian rite. But the water of baptism had no power there, where the spring of faith had not yet arisen within.

Yet herein also was he strong; more than a man's strength against the rival power of evil lay in his act, and as if it overwhelmed her, she dropped her arms, looked with a surprised glance and pale cheeks at him, who seemed a powerful sorcerer, strong in wizardry and secret lore. They were dark runes which he spoke, mystic signs which he was making in the air! She would not have blinked if he had swung an axe or a sharp knife before her eyes, but she did when he made the sign of the cross on her forehead and breast; she now sat like a tame bird, her head bowed down on her bosom.

Gently he told her of the work of love she had done for him in the night, that she had come in the hideous skin of a frog, and had loosed his bonds, and brought him out to light and life. He said that she also was bound—bound in a closer bondage than he had been, but she, too, with him should come to light and life. He would bring her to Haddeby, to the holy Anskarius. There, in the Christian city, the enchantment would be broken. But he would not dare to carry her in front of him on the horse, although she herself was willing to sit there.

"You must sit behind me on the horse, not in front of me! Thy witch-beauty has a power that is from the evil one. I dread it—and yet there is victory for me in Christ!"

He bent his knees and prayed gently and earnestly. It was as if the silent glades of the forest were consecrated thereby into a holy church. The birds began to sing as if they belonged to a new brotherhood; the mint poured forth its fragrance as if it would take the place of incense. The priest proclaimed aloud the words of Holy Writ:—

" 'The Dayspring from on high hath visited us, to give light to them that sit in darkness and in the shadow of death, and to guide our feet into the way of peace!' "

And he spoke about the longing of the whole Creation, and whilst he spoke the horse, which had carried them in its wild race, stood quiet, and shook the great brambles, so that the ripe, juicy berries fell on little Helga's hand, offering themselves for her refreshment.

Patiently she let herself be lifted on to the back of the horse, and sat there like one walks in his sleep, who is not awake, but yet is not moving in his dream. The Christian fastened two boughs together with a strip of bark to form a cross, and held it aloft in his hands. So they rode through the forest, which became denser as the way grew deeper, or rather, there was no way at all. Sloes grew across the path; one was obliged to ride around them. The spring did not become a running brook, but a standing bog, and one had to ride around that. There was strength and refreshment in the fresh forest air; there was not less power in the word of gentleness which sounded in faith and Christian love, in the heartfelt desire to bring the possessed to light and life.

They say that the drops of rain can hollow the hard stone, the billows of the sea can in time wear smooth the broken, sharp-edged pieces of rock. The dew of Grace, which had descended upon little Helga, pierced the hardness and rounded the ruggedness of her nature, although it was not yet evident, and she was not yet aware of it herself. But what does the germ in the earth know of the refreshing moisture and the warm rays of the sun, while yet it is hiding within itself plant and flower?

As a mother's song for her child imperceptibly fastens itself into its mind, and it babbles single words after her, without understanding them, although they afterwards collect themselves in its thoughts, and become clear in the course of time, so in her the Word worked which is able to create.

They rode out of the forest, away over the heath, again through pathless forest, and towards evening they met some robbers.

"Where have you stolen that fair maiden?" they shouted; they stopped the horse, and snatched the two riders from it, for they were strong men. The priest had no other weapon than the knife which he had taken from little Helga to defend himself with; one of the robbers swung his axe, but the young Christian avoided it, and lightly sprang aside, or he would have been struck; but the edge of the axe sank deep into the horse's neck, so that the blood streamed out, and the animal fell to the earth. Then little Helga started, as if awakened out of a long, deep meditation, and threw herself down on the expiring animal. The Christian priest placed himself before her in order to defend her, but one of the robbers dashed a ponderous iron mace against his forehead, crushing it. The blood and brains spurted around, and he fell dead to the earth.

The robbers seized little Helga by her white arm. At that moment the sun went down, and as the last ray faded, she was changed to a hideous toad. Her greenish mouth opened across half her face; her arms became thin and slimy, and her hands grew broad and covered with webbing. Terror seized the robbers at the sight. She stood among them, a hideous monster; then, frog-like, hopped away, with bounds higher than she was herself, and vanished in the thicket. The robbers knew it for an evil trick of Loge, or secret magic art, and hurried away in affright.

The full moon was already rising, and soon shone forth in splendor, and little Helga crept forth from the thicket in the skin of a wretched toad. She stood by the bodies of the Christian priest and of the horse, and she looked at them with eyes that seemed to weep. Her frog's head uttered a moan like a child beginning to cry. She threw herself now upon one, now upon the other; she took water in her hand, which the webbed skin had made larger and more hollow, and poured it over them. They were dead, and would remain dead; she understood that. Wild animals would soon come and devour their bodies; but that must not be! So she dug in the earth as deep as she could. To open a grave for them was her wish, but she had nothing to dig it with except a strong bough of a tree and her weak hands; but on them there was webbing stretched between her fingers. She tore it, and the blood flowed. These means would be of no use, she could see. Then she took water and washed the dead man's face, covered it with fresh green leaves, fetched great boughs and laid them over him, shook leaves between them, then took the heaviest stones she was able to lift, laid them over the dead bodies, and filled up the openings with moss. Then the mound seemed strong and protected, but this arduous task had occupied the entire night—the sun now burst forth, and little Helga stood in all her beauty, with bleeding hands, and, for the first time, with tears on her flushed maiden cheeks.

In this transformation, it seemed as if the two natures struggled within her. She trembled, and gazed around her as if she had awoke from a frightful dream. Running to a slender beech, she held fast to it for support, then climbed to the top of the tree, as lithely as a cat, and clung fast to it. There she sat like a frightened squirrel, sat there all through the long day in the deep solitude of the forest, where all is still and death-like as they say. Yet a pair of butterflies fluttered about at play or in quarrel; there were ant-hills close by with many hundreds of busy little creatures that crowded backwards and forwards. Countless gnats danced in the air, swarm upon swarm; hosts of buzzing flies chased each other about; birds, dragon-flies, and other small winged creatures filled the air. The earth-worm crept out from the moist soil, the mole raised itself above the ground. In all else it was still and death-like around, or what one calls death-like indeed! Nothing took any notice of little Helga, except the jays, which flew screaming around the top of the tree where she was sitting. They jumped along the branches near her in daring inquisitiveness. One glance of her eye was enough to chase them away again; but they could not quite make her out, neither could she understand herself.

When evening was near, and the sun began to go down, her approaching change called her to movement again. She let herself slide down from the tree, and when the last ray of the sun disappeared, she sat there in the toad's shrunken form, with the webbed skin of her hands lacerated, but her eyes now sparkled with a brilliancy of beauty which they had scarcely possessed before, even in her beautiful human shape. They were now the gentle eyes of a pious maiden that looked from behind the reptile's outward shape, and told of a deepened mind, of a true human heart. The beautiful eyes swam with tears, heavy tears that relieved her heart.

The cross of boughs bound together with a strip of bark, the last work of him who now lay dead and buried, was still lying on the grave she had made. Little Helga now took it, at some unprompted impulse, and planted it amongst the stones, over him and the slain horse. The sadness of the recollection brought tears to her eyes, and with the grief in her heart she traced the same sign in the earth around the grave that so honorably enclosed the dead. As with both hands she traced the sign of the cross, the webbing fell off like a torn glove! She washed herself in the water of the spring, and looked with astonishment at her fine white hands. Again she made the sign of the cross in the air between herself and the grave; her lips quivered, her tongue moved, and that Name, which she had heard pronounced most frequently on her ride through the forest, came audibly from her mouth—she said, "Jesus Christ!"

The toad's skin fell off: she was a beautiful young maiden; but her head drooped wearily, her limbs needed repose—she slept.

Her slumber was short; at midnight she awoke. The dead horse was standing before her, shining, and full of life, that gleamed in light from its eyes and from its wounded neck. Close by she saw the murdered Christian priest, "more beautiful than Baldur!" as the Viking's wife would have said; and he appeared surrounded with a glory of fire.

There was an earnest look in his large, gentle eyes, just and searching, so penetrating a gaze that it seemed to shine into the inmost recesses of her heart. Little Helga trembled before it, and her memory was awakened with a power as if it was the Day of Judgment. Every kind action that had been done for her, every kindly word that had been spoken to her, seemed endued with life; she understood that it was mercy which had taken care of her during her days of trial, in which the child of spirit and clay works and strives. She owned that she had only followed the bent of her own desire, and had done nothing on her own part. Everything had been given to her, everything had been allowed, so to speak. She bowed herself humbly, ashamed before Him who alone can read the hidden things of the heart; and in that instant there seemed to come to her a fiery touch of purifying flame—the flame of the Holy Spirit.

"Thou daughter of the mire," said the Christian priest, "from the mire, from the earth thou art sprung; from earth thou shalt again arise. The fire within thee returns in personality to its source; the ray is not from the sun, but from God. No soul shall perish, but far distant is the time when life shall be merged in eternity. I come from the land of the dead; so shalt thou at some time travel through the deep valley to the shining hill-country, where grace and fullness dwell. I may not lead thee to Hadde for Christian baptism. First thou must burst the water-shield over the deep moorland, and draw up the living root that gave thee life and cradled thee. Thou must do thy work before the consecration may come to thee."

And he lifted her on to the horse, handed her a golden censer, like that which she had seen in the Viking's castle, from which there came a sweet, strong fragrance. The open wound on the forehead of the slain shone like a radiant diadem. He took the cross from the grave, raised it on high; and now they went off through the air, over the rustling forest, then over the mounds where the warriors were buried, sitting on their dead steeds; and these majestic forms arose, and rode out to the tops of the hills. A broad golden hoop with a gold knob gleamed on their foreheads in the moonlight, and their cloaks fluttered in the wind. The dragon that sits and broods over treasure raised its head, and looked after them. Dwarfs peered forth from the hills, and the furrows swarmed with red, blue, and green lights, like a cluster of sparks in a burnt piece of paper.

Away over wood and heath, stream and pool, they flew to the moor, and floated over that in great circles. The Christian priest raised the cross on high; it shone like gold, and from his lips came the eucharistic chant. Little Helga sang with him, as a child joins in the song of its mother. She swung the censer, and there came a fragrance as if from an altar, so powerful, so subtly operating, that the rushes and reeds of the moor put forth their flowers. All the germs sprang up from the deep soil; everything that had life arose. A veil of water-lilies spread itself like an embroidered carpet of flowers, and on it lay a sleeping woman, young and beautiful. Little Helga thought she saw herself mirrored in the still water; but it was her mother that she saw, the Marsh King's wife, the princess from the waters of the Nile.

The dead Christian priest bade the sleeper be lifted on to the horse; but that sank under the burden as if its body was only a winding-sheet flying in the breeze; but the sign of the cross made the airy phantom strong, and all three rode to the firm ground.

A cock crowed in the Viking's stronghold. The phantoms rose up in the mist, and were dispersed in the wind, but mother and daughter stood there together.

"Is that myself that I see in the deep water?" said the mother.

"Is that myself that I see in the bright shield?" exclaimed the daughter; and they came close together, breast to breast in each other's arms. The mother's heart beat strongest, and she understood it all.

"My child! My own heart's flower! My lotus from the deep waters!"

And she embraced her child, and wept over her; and the tears were as a baptism of new life and affection for little Helga.

"I came hither in a swan's skin, and I took it off," said the mother. "I sank through the quivering swamp, deep into the mire of the bog, that enclosed me as with a wall. But soon I found a fresher current about me; a power seemed to draw me ever deeper and deeper. I felt a pressure of sleep on my eyelids; I slept, I dreamt—I seemed to lie again in the pyramids of Egypt; but there still stood before me the moving elder-stump, which had frightened me on the surface of the moor. I looked at the crevices in the bark, and they shone forth in colors and became hieroglyphics—it was the case of a mummy which I was looking at. That burst, and out of it stepped a lord a thousand years old, a mummy form, black as pitch, shining black like a wood-snail or the slimy black mud—the Marsh King, or the mummy of the pyramid, I did not know which. He flung his arms about me, and I felt that I should die. When I first returned to life again, and my breast became warm, there was a little bird which beat its wings, and twittered and sang. It flew up from my breast towards the dark, heavy roof, but a long green band still fastened it to me. I heard and understood its longing notes: 'Liberty! sunshine! to my father!' Then I thought of my father in the sun-lit land of my home, my life, my affection! and I loosed the band and let him flutter away—home to his father. Since that hour I have not dreamed; I slept a long and heavy sleep till the moment when the sounds and fragrance arose and raised me."

That green band from the mother's heart to the bird's wings, whither had it passed now? where was it lying cast away? Only the stork had seen it. The band was that green stalk; the knot was that shining flower which served as a cradle for the child who now had grown in beauty, and again reposed near the mother's heart.

And whilst they stood there in close embrace, the father-stork flew in circles about them, made speed to his nest, fetched from

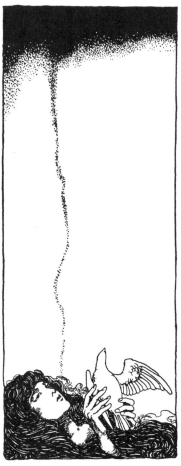

There was a little bird that
beat its wings

thence the feather-dresses kept for so many years and threw one over each of them; and they flew, and raised themselves from the earth like two white swans.

"Let us talk," said father-stork, "now that we can understand each other's speech, although the beak is cut differently on one bird and on the other! It is the most lucky thing possible that you came to-night. In the morning we should have been off, mother, and I, and the young ones! We are flying to the South! Yes, look at me! I am an old friend from the land of the Nile, and that is the mother; she has more in her heart than in her chatter. She always believed that the princess was only taking care of herself. I and the young ones have brought the swan-skins here. Well, how glad I am! And what a fortunate thing it is that I am here still! At daybreak we shall set off, a large party of storks. We fly in front; you can fly behind, and then you will not mistake the way. I and the young ones will then be able to keep an eye upon you!"

"And the lotus flower, that I ought to bring," said the Egyptian princess, "it flies in swan's plumage by my side! I have the flower of my heart with me; thus it has released itself. Homeward! homeward!"

But Helga said that she could not leave the land of Denmark till she had once more seen her foster-mother, the kind wife of the Viking. In Helga's thoughts came up every beautiful remembrance, every affectionate word, every tear which her foster-mother had shed, and it almost seemed at that instant as if she clung closest to that mother.

"Yes, we will go to the Viking's house," said the stork-father. "There I expect mother and the young ones. How they will open their eyes and chatter about it! Yes, mother doesn't say so very much; what she does is short and pithy, and so she thinks the best! I will sound the rattle directly, so that she will hear we are coming."

And so father-stork chattered his beak, and flew with the swans to the Viking's stronghold.

Every one there was lying deep in slumber. The Viking's wife had not gone to rest till late that night; she was still in fear for little Helga, who had disappeared three days ago with the Christian priest. She must have helped him to escape, for it was her horse that was missing from the stable. By what power had all this been brought about? The Viking's wife thought about the wonderful works which she had heard were performed by the White Christ, and by those who believed in Him and followed Him. Her changing thoughts shaped themselves into a dream. It appeared to her that she was still sitting on her bed, awake, and meditating, and that darkness shrouded everything outside. A storm arose; she heard the rolling of the sea in the west and the east, from the North Sea and the waters of the Cattegat. That huge serpent which encircles the earth in the depths of the ocean shook convulsively; it was Ragnarök, the twilight of the gods, as the heathen called the last hour, when everything should pass away, even the high gods themselves. The trumpet sounded, and the gods rode forth over the rainbow, arrayed in steel, to take part in the last contest. Before them flew the winged warrior-maidens, and behind them in array marched the forms of dead warriors. The whole sky was illuminated by the northern lights, but the darkness again prevailed. It was an appalling hour.

And close by the frightened Viking's wife little Helga sat on the floor in the hideous form of a toad, trembling and nestling herself up against her foster-mother, who took her on her lap and affectionately held her fast, although she seemed more hideous than a toad. The air was full of the sound of sword-strokes and the blows of maces, of arrows whizzing, as if a furious hail-storm was raging above them. The hour had come when earth and heaven should fail, the stars should fall, and everything be burned up in the fire of Surtr; but the dreamer knew that a new earth and heaven would come, and the corn wave where the sea now rolled over the barren sand bottom; that the God who cannot be named rules, and up to Him rose Baldur, the gentle and kind, loosed from the realm of death. He came—the Viking's wife saw him, and knew his face. It was the captive Christian priest.

"White Christ!" she cried aloud; and as she mentioned that Name she pressed a kiss on the hideous forehead of her frog-child; the toad's skin fell off, and little Helga stood there in all her beauty, gentle as she had never been before, and with beaming eyes. She kissed her foster-mother's hands, blessed her for all her care and affection with which she had surrounded her in the days of her distress and trial; thanked her for the thoughts to which she had given birth in her; thanked her for mentioning the Name which she repeated, "White Christ!" and then little Helga rose up as a noble swan, her wings expanded themselves wide, wide, with a rustling as when a flock of birds of passage flies away!

With that the Viking's wife awoke, and still heard outside the same strong sound of wings. She knew that it was time for the storks to depart, and no doubt that was what she heard. Still, she wished to see them once before their journey, and to bid them farewell. She stood up, went out on to the balcony, and there she saw on the ridge of the out-house rows of storks, and round the courtyard and over the lofty trees crowds of others were flying in great circles. But straight in front of her, on the edge of the well, where little Helga had so often sat and frightened her with her wildness, two swans now sat and looked at her with intelligent eyes. Her dream came to her mind; it still quite filled her as if it had been reality. She thought of little Helga in the form of a swan, she thought of the Christian priest, and she felt a strange joy in her heart.

The swans beat their wings, and bent their necks, as if they wished so to salute her; and the Viking's wife stretched out her arms towards them as if she understood, and smiled at them through her tears.

Then, with a noise of wings and chattering, all the storks arose to start on their journey to the south.

"We cannot wait for the swans!" said mother-stork. "If they wish to come with us they may; but we can't wait here till the plovers start! It is a very good thing to travel in family parties; not like the chaffinches and ruffs, where the males fly by themselves and the females by themselves; that is certainly not proper! And what are those swans flapping their wings for?"

"Every one flies in his own way!" said father-stork. "The swans go in slanting line, the cranes in a triangle, and the plovers in a wavy, snake-like line."

"Don't mention serpents when we are flying up here!" said mother-stork; "it only excites the appetites of our young ones when they can't be satisfied."

"Are those the high mountains down there which I have heard of?" asked Helga in the swan's skin.

"Those are thunder-clouds which drive below us," said the mother.

"What are those white clouds which lift themselves so high?" asked Helga.

"Those are the everlasting snow-clad hills which you see," said the mother; and they flew over the Alps, down towards the blue Mediterranean.

"Land of Africa! Coast of Egypt!" jubilantly sang the daughter of the Nile in her swan form, when, high in the air, she descried her native land, like a yellowish white, undulating streak.

And as the birds saw it, they hastened their flight.

"I smell the mud of the Nile and the wet frogs!" said mother-stork. "It quite excites me! Yes, now you shall taste them; now you shall see the adjutant bird, the ibis, and the cranes! They all belong to our family, but they are not nearly so handsome as we are. They stick themselves up, especially the ibis; he is now quite pampered by the Egyptians—they make a mummy of him, and stuff him with aromatic herbs. I would rather be stuffed with live frogs, and so would you, and so you shall be. It is better to have something inside you while you live than to be in state when you are dead! That is my opinion, and that is always right!"

"Now the storks are come!" they said in the rich house on the bank of the Nile, where, in the open hall on soft cushions covered with a leopard's skin, the royal master lay outstretched, neither living nor dead, hoping for the lotus flower from the deep marsh in the north. Kinsmen and servants stood around him.

And into the hall flew two beautiful white swans, which had come with the storks! They threw off their dazzling feather-dress, and there stood two beautiful women, as much alike as two drops of dew! They bent down over the pale, withered old man; they put back their long hair, and when little Helga stooped over her grandfather, the color returned to his cheeks, his eyes sparkled, and life came into his stiffened limbs. The old man raised himself healthy and vigorous; daughter and granddaughter held him in their arms as if they were giving him a morning salutation in their joy after a long, heavy dream.

And there was joy over all the house and in the storks' nest, but there it was chiefly over the good food, and the swarming hosts of frogs; and whilst the learned men made haste to note down in brief the history of the two princesses and the flower of health, which was such a great event and a blessing for house and country, the parent storks related it in their fashion to their own family, but not till they had all satisfied their hunger, or else they would have had something else to do than to listen to stories.

"Now you will become somebody!" whispered mother-stork; "that is certain!"

"Well! what should I become?" said father-stork; "and what have I done? A mere nothing!"

"You have done more than all the others! But for you and the young ones the two princesses would never have seen Egypt again, and made the old man well. You will become somebody! You will certainly receive a Doctor's degree, and our young ones will bear it afterwards, and their young ones will have it in turn. You look already like an Egyptian doctor—in my eyes!"

The wise and learned expounded the fundamental idea, as they called it, that ran through the whole history: "Love brings forth life!"—they gave that explanation in different ways—"the warm sunbeam was the Egyptian princess, she descended to the Marsh King, and in their meeting the flower sprang forth—"

"I can't repeat the words quite right," said father-stork, who had heard it from the roof, and was expected to tell them all about it in his nest. "What they said was so involved, it was so clever, that they immediately received honors and gifts. Even the head cook obtained a high mark of distinction—that was for the soup!"

"And what did you receive?" inquired mother-stork; "they ought not to forget the most important, and that is yourself. The learned have only chattered about it all, but your turn will come!"

Late that night, while peaceful slumber enwrapped the now prosperous house, there was one who was still awake; and that was not the father-stork, though he stood on one leg in the nest and slept like a sentinel. No, little Helga was awake. She leaned out over the balcony and gazed at the clear sky, with the great, bright stars, larger and purer in their luster than she had seen them in the north, and yet the same. She thought of the Viking's wife by the moor, of her foster-mother's gentle eyes, and the tears she had shed over her poor toad-child, who now stood in the light and splendor of the stars by the waters of the Nile in the soft air of spring. She thought of the love in that heathen woman's breast, that love which she had shown to a miserable creature who, in human form, was an evil brute, and in the form of an animal, loathsome to look at and to touch. She looked at the shining stars, and called to mind the splendor on the forehead of the dead man, when they flew away over forest and moor; tones resounded in her recollection, words she had heard pronounced when they rode away, and she sat as if paralyzed—words about the great Author of Love, the highest Love, embracing all generations.

Yes, how much had been given, gained, obtained! Little Helga's thoughts were occupied, night and day, with all her good fortune, and she stood in contemplation of it like a child which turns quickly from the giver to all the beautiful presents that have been given; so she rose up in her increasing happiness, which could come and would come. She was indeed borne in mysterious ways to even higher joy and happiness, and in this she lost herself one day so entirely that she thought no more of the Giver. It was the strength of youthful courage that inspired her bold venture. Her eyes shone, but suddenly she was called back by a great clamor in the courtyard beneath. There she saw two powerful ostriches running hurriedly about in narrow circles. She had never before seen that creature, so great a bird, so clumsy and heavy. Its wings looked as if they were clipped, the bird itself as if it had been injured, and she inquired what had been done to it, and for the first time heard the tradition which the Egyptians relate about the ostrich.

The race had at one time been beautiful, its wings large and powerful; then, one evening, a mighty forest bird said to it: "Brother, shall we fly to the river in the morning, if God will, and drink?" And the ostrich replied: "I will." When day broke they flew off, at first high up towards the sun—the eye of God—ever higher and higher, the ostrich far before all the others; it flew in its pride towards the light; it relied on its own strength, and not on the Giver; it did not say, "If God will!" Then the avenging angel drew back the veil from the burning flame, and in that instant the bird's wings were burnt; it sank miserably to the earth. Its descendants are no longer able to raise themselves; they fly in terror, rush about in circles in that narrow space. It is a reminder to us men, in all our thoughts, in all our actions, to say: "If God will!"

And Helga thoughtfully bowed her head, looked at the hurrying ostrich, saw its fear, saw its silly delight at the sight of its own great shadow on the white sunlit wall. And deep seriousness fixed itself into her mind and thoughts. So rich a life, so full of prosperity, was given, was obtained—what would happen? What was yet to come? The best thing: "If God will!"

In the early spring, when the storks again started for the north, little Helga took her gold bracelet, scratched her name on it, beckoned to the stork-father, placed the golden circlet about his neck, and asked him to bear it to the Viking's wife, by which she would understand that her foster-daughter was alive, and that she was happy, and thought of her.

Placed the golden circlet about his neck

"That is heavy to carry!" thought the father-stork when it was placed around his neck; "but one does not throw gold and honor on the high-road. They will find it true up there that the stork brings fortune!"

"You lay gold, and I lay eggs!" said the mother-stork; "but you only lay once, and I lay every year! But it vexes me that neither of us is appreciated."

"But we are quite aware of it ourselves, mother!" said father-stork.

"But you can't hang that on you," said mother-stork. "It neither gives us fair wind nor food."

And so they flew.

The little nightingale, that sang in the tamarind-bush, also wished to start for the north immediately. Little Helga had often heard him up there near the moor; she wished to give him a message, for she understood the speech of birds when she flew in the swan's skin, and she had often since that time used it with the stork and the swallow. The nightingale would understand her, and she asked him to fly to the beech-forest on the peninsula of Jutland, where she had erected the grave of stones and boughs; there she asked him to bid all the small birds to protect the grave, and always to sing their songs around it. And the nightingale flew—and time flew also.

The eagle stood on the pyramid in the autumn, and saw a magnificent array of richly laden camels, with armed men in costly clothing, on snorting Arabian steeds, shining as white as silver, and with red quivering nostrils, their heavy thick manes hanging down about their slender legs. Rich visitors, a royal prince from

She understood the speech of birds

the land of Arabia, beautiful as a prince ought to be, came to that noble house, where the storks' nest now stood empty, its former occupants now far away in the northern land, but soon to return. And they came exactly on that day which was most filled with joy and mirth. There was a grand wedding, and little Helga was the bride arrayed in silk and jewels; the bridegroom was the young prince from the land of Arabia; and the two sat highest at the table between the mother and grandfather. But she did not look at the bridegroom's brown, manly cheek, where his black beard curled; she did not look at his dark, fiery eyes, which were fastened upon her; she looked outwards and upwards towards the twinkling, sparkling stars, which beamed down from heaven.

Then there was a rustling sound of strong wing-strokes outside in the air—the storks had returned; and the old couple, however tired they might be with the journey, and however much they needed rest, still flew on to the railing of the verandah immediately they were aware whose festivity it was. They had already heard, at the frontier of the country, that little Helga had allowed them to be painted on the wall because they belonged to her history.

"That is very nicely borne in mind," said father-stork.

"It is very little!" said the stork-mother; "she could not have done less."

And when Helga saw them, she got up and went out into the verandah to them to pat them on the back. The old storks curtsied with their necks, and the youngest of their young ones looked on, and felt themselves honored.

And Helga looked up to the bright stars which shone clearer and clearer; and between them and her a form seemed to move still purer than the air, and seen through it, that hovered quite near her—it was the dead Christian priest; so he came on the day of her festivity, came from the Kingdom of Heaven.

"The splendor and glory which are there surpass every thing that earth knows!" he said.

And little Helga prayed gently and from her heart, as she had never prayed before, that she only for one single minute might dare to look within, might only cast one single glance into the Kingdom of Heaven, to the Father of all.

And he raised her into the splendor and glory, in one current of sounds and thoughts; it was not only round about her that it shone and sounded, but within her. No words are able to describe it.

"Now we must return; you are wanted!" he said.

"Only one glance more!" she entreated; "only one short minute!"

"We must go back to the earth; all the guests have gone away."

"Only one glance! the last—"

And little Helga stood outside in the verandah; but all the torches outside were extinguished, all the lights in the wedding chamber were gone, the storks were gone, no guests to be seen, no bridegroom; everything seemed to be blown away in three short minutes.

Then Helga was filled with terror, and she went through the great, empty hall, into the next room. Strange soldiers were sleeping there. She opened a side door that led into her apartment, and when she expected to stand there, she found herself outside in the garden; but it was not like this before—the heaven was red and shining, it was towards daybreak.

Only three minutes in Heaven, and a whole night had passed on the earth!

Then she saw the storks; she cried to them, speaking their language, and father-stork turned his head, listened, and drew near her.

"You are speaking our language!" said he; "what do you want? Why do you come here, you strange woman?"

"It is I! it is Helga! Don't you know me? Three minutes ago we were talking together, yonder in the verandah."

"That is a mistake!" said the stork; "you must have dreamt it!"

Then she saw the storks

"No, no!" she said, and reminded him of the Viking's stronghold and the moor, and of the journey hither!

Then father-stork blinked his eyes: "That is a very old story; I have heard it from my great-great-great-grand-mother's time! Yes, certainly, there was such a princess in Egypt from the land of Denmark, but she disappeared on the night of her wedding many hundreds of years ago, and never came back again. That you may read for yourself on the monument in the garden; there are sculptured both swans and storks, and at the top you yourself stand in white marble."

It was indeed so. Little Helga saw it, understood it, and fell on her knees.

The sun broke forth, and as in former times at the touch of its beams the toad form disappeared and the beautiful shape was seen, so she raised herself now at the baptism of light in a form of brighter beauty, purer than the air, a ray of light—to the Father of all.

Her body sank in dust; there lay a faded lotus-flower where she had stood.

Then that was a new ending to the story!" said the father-stork. "I had not at all expected it! but I rather like it!"

"I wonder what my young ones will say about it!" said the mother-stork.

"Yes, that is certainly the principal thing!" answered the father.

Father-stork

THE STORKS

N THE ROOF OF A HOUSE SITUATED AT THE EXTREMITY OF A small town, a stork had built his nest. There sat the mother-stork, with her four young ones, who all stretched out their little black bills, which had not yet become red. Not far off, upon the parapet, erect and proud, stood the father-stork; he had drawn one of his legs under him, being weary of standing on two. You might have fancied him carved in wood, he stood so motionless. "It looks so grand," thought he, "for my wife to have a sentinel to keep guard over her nest; people cannot know that I am her husband, they will certainly think that I am commanded to stand here—how well it looks!" and so he remained standing on one leg.

In the street below, a number of children were playing together. When they saw the storks, one of the liveliest amongst them began to sing as much as he could remember of some old rhymes about storks, in which he was soon joined by the others—

"Stork! stork! long-legged stork!
Into thy nest I prithee walk;
There sits thy mate,
With her four children so great.

> "The first we'll hang like a cat,
> The second we'll burn,
> The third on a spit well turn,
> The fourth drown dead as a rat!"

"Only listen to what the boys are singing," said the little storks; "they say we shall be hanged and burnt!"

"Never mind," said the mother, "don't listen to them; they will do you no harm."

But the boys went on singing, and pointed their fingers at the storks: only one little boy, called Peter, said "it was a sin to mock and tease animals, and that he would have nothing to do with it."

The mother-stork again tried to comfort her little ones. "Never mind," said she; "see how composedly your father is standing there, and upon one leg only."

"But we are so frightened!" said the young ones, drawing their heads down into the nest.

The next day, when the children were again assembled to play together, and saw the storks, they again began their song—

> "The first we'll hang like a cat,
> The second we'll burn!"

"And are we really to be hanged and burnt?" asked the young storks.

"No indeed!" said the mother. "You shall learn to fly: I will teach you myself. Then we can fly over to the meadow, and pay a visit to the frogs. They will bow to us in the water, and say, 'Croak, croak!' and then we shall eat them; will not that be nice?"

"And what then?" asked the little storks.

"Then all the storks in the country will gather together, and the autumnal exercise will begin. It is of the greatest consequence that you should fly well then; for every one who does not, the general will stab to death with his bill; so you must pay great attention when we begin to drill you, and learn very quickly."

"Then we shall really be killed after all, as the boys said? Oh, listen! they are singing it again!"

"Attend to me, and not to them!" said the mother. "After the grand exercise, we shall fly to warm countries, far, far away from here, over mountains and forests. We shall fly to Egypt, where are the three-cornered stone houses whose summits reach the clouds; they are called pyramids, and are older than it is possible for storks to imagine. There is a river too, which overflows its banks, so as to make the whole country like a marsh, and we shall go into the marsh and eat frogs."

"Oh!" said the young ones.

"Yes, it is delightful! one does nothing but eat all the day long. And whilst we are so comfortable, in this country not a single green leaf is left on the trees, and it is so cold that the clouds are frozen, and fall down upon the earth in little white pieces."—She meant snow, but she could not express herself more clearly.

"And will the naughty boys be frozen to pieces too?" asked the young storks.

"No, they will not be frozen to pieces; but they will be nearly as badly off as if they were; they will be obliged to crowd round the fire in their little dark rooms; while you, on the contrary, will be flying about in foreign lands, where there are beautiful flowers and warm sunshine."

Well, time passed away, and the young storks grew so tall, that when they stood upright in the nest they could see the country around to a great distance. The father-stork used to bring them every day the nicest little frogs, as well as snails, and all the other stork tit-bits he could find. Oh! it was so droll to see him show them his tricks; he would lay his head upon his tail, make a rattling noise with his bill, and then tell them such charming stories all about the moors.

"Now you must learn to fly!" said the mother one day; and accordingly, all the four young storks were obliged to come out upon the parapet. Oh, how they trembled! And though they balanced themselves on their wings, they were very near falling.

"Only look at me," said the mother. "This is the way you must hold your heads; and in this manner place your feet,—one, two! one, two! this will help you to get on." She flew a little way, and the young ones made an awkward spring after her,—bounce! down they fell; for their bodies were heavy.

"I will not fly," said one of the young ones, as he crept back into the nest. "I do not want to go into the warm countries!"

"Do you want to be frozen to death during the winter? Shall the boys come, and hang, burn, or roast you? Wait a little, I will call them!"

"Oh no!" said the little stork; and again he began to hop about on the roof like the others. By the third day they could fly pretty well, and so they thought they could also sit and take their ease in the air; but bounce! down they tumbled, and found themselves obliged to make use of their wings. The boys now came into the street, singing their favorite song—

"Stork! stork! long-legged stork!"

"Shall not we fly down and peck out their eyes?" said the young ones.

"No, leave them alone!" said the mother. "Attend to me, that is of much more importance!—one, two, three, now to the right!—one, two, three, now to the left, round the chimney-pot! That was very well; you managed your wings so neatly last time, that I will permit you to come with me to-morrow to the marsh: several first-rate stork families will be there with their children. Let it be said that mine are the prettiest and best behaved of all; and remember to stand very upright, and to throw out your chest; that looks well, and gives such an air of distinction!"

"Stork! stork! long-legged stork!"

"But are we not to take revenge upon those rude boys?" asked the young ones.

"Let them screech as much as they please! You will fly among the clouds, you will go to the land of the pyramids, when they must shiver with cold, and have not a single green leaf to look at, nor a single sweet apple to eat!"

"Yes, we shall be revenged!" whispered they one to another. And then they were drilled again.

Of all the boys in the town, the forwardest in singing nonsensical verses was always the same one who had begun teasing the storks, a little urchin not more than six years old. The young storks indeed fancied him a hundred years old, because he was bigger than either their father or mother, and what should they know about the ages of children, or grown up human beings! All their schemes of revenge were aimed at this little boy; he had been the first to tease them, and continued to do so. The young storks were highly excited about it, and the older they grew, the less they were inclined to endure persecution. Their mother, in order to pacify them, at last promised that they should be revenged, but not until the last day of their stay in this place.

"We must first see how you behave your selves at the grand exercise; if then you should fly badly, and the general should thrust his beak into your breast, the boys will, in some measure, be proved in the right. Let me see how well you will behave!"

"Yes, that you shall!" said the young ones. And now they really took great pains, practiced every day, and at last flew so lightly and prettily, that it was a pleasure to see them.

Well, now came the autumn. All the storks assembled, in order to fly together to warm countries for the winter. What a practicing there was! Away they went over woods and fields, towns and villages, merely to see how well they could fly, for they had a long journey before them. The young storks distinguished themselves so honorably that they were pronounced "worthy of frogs and serpents." This was the highest character they could obtain; now they were allowed to eat frogs and serpents, and accordingly they did eat them.

And fetch one for each of the boys

"Now we will have our revenge!" said they.

"Very well!" said the mother; "I have been thinking what will be the best. I know where the pool is in which all the little human children lie until the storks come and take them to their parents: the pretty little things sleep and dream so pleasantly as they will never dream again. All parents like to have a little child, and all children like to have a little brother or sister. We will fly to the pool and fetch one for each of the boys who has not sung that wicked song, nor made a jest of the storks; and the other naughty children shall have none."

"But he who first sung those naughty rhymes! that great ugly fellow! what shall we do to him?" cried the young storks.

"In the pool there lies a little child who has dreamed away his life; we will take it for

PLATE 9.
"We will bring him two little ones, a brother
and a sister"

him, and he will weep because he has only a little dead brother. But as to the good boy who said it was a sin to mock and tease animals, surely you have not forgotten him? We will bring him two little ones, a brother and a sister. And as this little boy's name is Peter, you too shall for the future be called 'Peter!'"

And it came to pass just as the mother said; and all the storks were called "Peter," and are still so called to this very day.

He would say, "Oh! how pretty that is!"

The Nightingale

IN CHINA, AS YOU WELL KNOW, THE EMPEROR IS CHINESE, and all around him are Chinese also. Now what I am about to relate happened many years ago, but even on that very account it is the more important that you should hear the story now, before it is forgotten.

The Emperor's palace was the most magnificent palace in the world; it was made entirely of fine porcelain, exceedingly costly; but at the same time so brittle, that it was dangerous even to touch it.

The choicest flowers were to be seen in the garden; and to the most splendid of all these little silver bells were fastened, in order that their tinkling might prevent any one from passing by without noticing them. Yes! everything in the Emperor's garden was excellently well arranged; and the garden extended so far, that even the gardener did not know the end of it; whoever walked beyond it, however, came to a beautiful wood, with very high trees; and beyond that, to the sea. The wood went down quite to the sea, which was very deep and blue; large ships could sail close under the branches; and among the branches dwelt a nightingale, who sang so sweetly, that even the poor fisherman, who had so

Among the branches dwelt
a nightingale

much else to do, when he came out at night-time to cast his nets, would stand still and listen to her song. "Oh! how pretty that is!" he would say—but then he was obliged to mind his work, and forget the bird; yet the following night, if again the nightingale sang, and the fisherman came out, again he would say, "Oh! how pretty that is!"

Travellers came from all parts of the world to the Emperor's city; and they admired the city, the palace, and the garden; but if they heard the nightingale, they all said, "This is the best." And they talked about her after they went home, and learned men wrote books about the city, the palace, and the garden; nor did they forget the nightingale: she was extolled above everything else; and poets wrote the most beautiful verses about the nightingale of the wood near the sea.

These books went round the world, and one of them at last reached the Emperor. He was sitting in his golden arm-chair; he

They admired the city, the palace, and the garden

read and read, and nodded his head every moment; for these splendid descriptions of the city, the palace, and the garden pleased him greatly. "But the nightingale is the best of all," was written in the book.

"What in the world is this?" said the Emperor. "The nightingale! I do not know it at all! Can there be such a bird in my empire, in my garden even, without my having even heard of it? Truly one may learn something from books."

So he called his Cavalier (that is, his gentleman in waiting); now this was so grand a personage, that no one of inferior rank might speak to him; and if one did venture to ask him a question, his only answer was "Pish!" which has no particular meaning.

"There is said to be a very remarkable bird here, called the nightingale," said the Emperor; "her song, they say, is worth more than anything else in all my dominions; why has no one ever told me of her?"

"I have never before heard her mentioned," said the Cavalier; "she has never been presented at court."

"I wish her to come, and sing before me this evening," said the Emperor. "The whole world knows what I have, and I do not know it myself!"

"I have never before heard her mentioned," said the Cavalier, "but I will seek her, I will find her."

But where was she to be found? The Cavalier ran up one flight of steps, down another, through halls, and through passages; not one of all whom he met had ever heard of the nightingale; and the Cavalier returned to the Emperor, and said, "It must certainly be an invention of the man who wrote the book. Your Imperial Majesty must not believe all that is written in books;

much in them is pure invention, and there is what is called the Black Art."

"But the book in which I have read it," said the Emperor, "was sent me by the high and mighty Emperor of Japan, and therefore it cannot be untrue. I wish to hear the nightingale; she must be here this evening, and if she do not come, after supper the whole court shall be flogged."

"Tsing-pe!" said the Cavalier; and again he ran upstairs, and downstairs, through halls, and through passages, and half the court ran with him; for not one would have relished the flogging. Many were the questions asked respecting the wonderful nightingale, whom the whole world talked of, and about whom no one at court knew anything.

At last they met a poor little girl in the kitchen, who said, "Oh yes! the nightingale! I know her very well. Oh! how she can sing! Every evening I carry the fragments left at table to my poor sick mother. She lives by the sea-shore; and when I am coming back, and stay to rest a little in the wood, I hear the nightingale sing; it makes the tears come into my eyes! it is just as if my mother kissed me."

"Little kitchen maiden," said the Cavalier, "I will procure for you a sure appointment in the kitchen, together with permission to see His Majesty the Emperor dine, if you will conduct us to the nightingale, for she is expected at court this evening."

So they went together to the wood, where the nightingale was accustomed to sing; and half the court went with them. Whilst on their way, a cow began to low.

"Oh!" said the court pages, "now we have her! It is certainly an extraordinary voice for so small an animal; surely I have heard it somewhere before."

The little kitchen-maid

"No, those are cows you hear lowing," said the little kitchen-maid, "we are still far from the place."

The frogs were now croaking in the pond.

"That is famous!" said the chief court-preacher, "now I hear her; it sounds just like little church-bells."

"No, those are frogs," said the little kitchen-maid, "but now I think we shall soon hear her."

Then began the nightingale to sing.

"There she is!" said the little girl. "Listen! listen! there she sits," and she pointed to a little grey bird up in the branches.

"Is it possible?" said the Cavalier. "I should not have thought it. How simple she looks! she must certainly have changed color at the sight of so many distinguished personages."

"Little nightingale!" called out the kitchen-maid, "our gracious Emperor wishes you to sing something to him."

"With the greatest pleasure," said the nightingale, and she sang in such a manner that it was delightful to hear her.

"It sounds like glass bells," said the Cavalier. "And look at her little throat, how it moves! It is singular that we should

PLATE 10.
Then began the nightingale to sing

never have heard her before; she will have great success at court."

"Shall I sing again to the Emperor?" asked the nightingale, for she thought the Emperor was among them.

"Most excellent nightingale!" said the Cavalier, "I have the honor to invite you to a court festival, which is to take place this evening, when His Imperial Majesty will be enchanted with your delightful song."

"My song would sound far better among the green trees," said the nightingale; however, she followed willingly when she heard that the Emperor wished it.

There was a regular trimming and polishing at the palace; the walls and the floors, which were all of porcelain, glittered with a thousand gold lamps; the loveliest flowers, with the merriest tinkling bells, were placed in the passages; there was a running to and fro, which made all the bells to ring, so that one could not hear his own words.

In the midst of the grand hall where the Emperor sat, a golden perch was erected, on which the nightingale was to sit. The whole court was present, and the little kitchen-maid received permission to stand behind the door, for she had now actually the rank and title of "Maid of the Kitchen." All were dressed out in their finest clothes; and all eyes were fixed upon the little grey bird, to whom the Emperor nodded as a signal for her to begin.

And the nightingale sang so sweetly, that tears came into the Emperor's eyes, tears rolled down his cheeks; and the nightingale sang more sweetly still, and touched the hearts of all who heard her; and the Emperor was so merry, that he said, "The nightingale should have his golden slippers, and wear them round her neck."

But the nightingale thanked him, and said she was already sufficiently rewarded.

"I have seen tears in the Emperor's eyes; that is the greatest reward I can have. The tears of an Emperor have a particular value. Heaven knows I am sufficiently rewarded." And then she sang again with her sweet, lovely voice.

"It is the most amiable coquetry ever known," said the ladies present; and they put water into their mouths, and tried to move their throats as she did when they spoke; they thought to become nightingales also. Indeed even the footmen and chamber-maids declared that they were quite contented; which was a great thing to say, for of all people they are the most difficult to satisfy. Yes indeed! the nightingale's success was complete. She was now to remain at court, to have her own cage; with permission to fly out twice in the day, and once in the night. Twelve attendants were allotted her, who were to hold a silken band, fastened round her foot; and they kept good hold. There was no pleasure in excursions made in this manner.

All the city was talking of the wonderful bird; and when two persons met, one would say only "night," and the other "gale," and then they sighed, and understood each other perfectly; indeed eleven of the children of the citizens were named after the nightingale, but none of them had her tones in their throats.

One day a large parcel arrived for the Emperor, on which was written "Nightingale."

"Here we have another new book about our far-famed bird," said the Emperor. But it was not a book; it was a little piece of mechanism, lying in a box; an artificial nightingale, which was intended to look like the living one, but was covered all over with diamonds, rubies, and sapphires. When this artificial bird had been wound up, it could sing one of the tunes that the real nightingale sang; and its tail, all glittering with silver and gold, went up and down all the time. A little band was fastened round its neck, on which was written, "The nightingale of the Emperor of China is poor compared with the nightingale of the Emperor of Japan."

"That is famous!" said every one; and he who had brought the bird obtained the title of "Chief Imperial Nightingale Bringer." "Now they shall sing together; we will have a duet."

And so they must sing together; but it did not succeed, for the real nightingale sang in her own way, and the artificial bird produced its tones by wheels. "It is not his fault," said the artist, "he keeps exact time and quite according to method."

The Chief Imperial
Nightingale Bringer

He was quite as successful as the real nightingale

So the artificial bird must now sing alone; he was quite as successful as the real nightingale; and then he was so much prettier to look at; his plumage sparkled like jewels.

Three and thirty times he sang one and the same tune, and yet he was not weary; every one would willingly have heard him again; however, the Emperor now wished the real nightingale should sing something—but where was she? No one had remarked that she had flown out of the open window; flown away to her own green wood.

"What is the meaning of this?" said the Emperor; and all the courtiers abused the nightingale, and called her a most ungrateful creature. "We have the best bird at all events," said they, and for the four and thirtieth time they heard the same tune, but still they did not quite know it, because it was so difficult. The artist praised the bird inordinately; indeed he declared it was superior to the real nightingale, not only in its exterior, all sparkling with diamonds, but also intrinsically.

"For see, my noble lords, his Imperial Majesty especially, with the real nightingale, one could never reckon on what was coming; but everything is settled with the artificial bird; he will sing in this one way, and no other: this can be proved, he can be taken to pieces, and the works can be shown, where the wheels lie, how they move, and how one follows from another."

"That is just what I think," said everybody; and the artist received permission to show the bird to the people on the following Sunday. "They too should hear him sing," the Emperor said. So they heard him, and were as well pleased as if they had all been drinking tea; for it is tea that makes Chinese merry, and they all said oh! and raised their fore-fingers, and nodded their heads. But the fisherman, who had heard the real nightingale, said, "It sounds very pretty, almost like the real bird; but yet there is something wanting, I do not know what."

The real nightingale was, however, banished the empire.

The artificial bird had his place on a silken cushion, close to the Emperor's bed; all the presents he received, gold and precious stones, lay around him; he had obtained the rank and title of "High Imperial Dessert Singer," and, therefore, his place was number one on the left side; for the Emperor thought that the side where the heart was situated must be the most honorable, and the heart is situated on the left side of an Emperor, as well as with other folks.

And the artist wrote five and twenty volumes about the artificial bird, with the longest and most difficult words that are to be found in the Chinese language. So, of course, all said they had read and understood them, otherwise they would have been stupid, and perhaps would have been flogged.

Thus it went on for a year. The Emperor, the court, and all the Chinese knew every note of the artificial bird's song by heart; but that was the very reason they enjoyed it so much, they could now sing with him. The little boys in the street sang "Zizizi, cluck, cluck, cluck!" and the Emperor himself sang too—yes indeed, that was charming!

But one evening, when the bird was in full voice, and the Emperor lay in bed, and listened, there was suddenly a noise, "bang," inside the bird, then something sprang "fur-r-r-r," all the wheels were running about, and the music stopped.

The Emperor jumped quickly out of bed, and had his chief physician called; but of what use could he be? Then a clockmaker was fetched, and at last, after a great deal of discussion and consultation, the bird was in some measure put to rights again; but the clockmaker said he must be spared much singing, for the pegs were almost worn out, and it was impossible to renew them, at least so that the music should be correct.

There was great lamentation, for now the artificial bird was allowed to sing only once a year, and even then there were difficulties; however, the artist made a short speech full of his favorite long words, and said the bird was as good as ever: so then, of course, it was as good as ever.

When five years were passed away, a great affliction visited the whole empire, for in their hearts the people thought highly of their Emperor; and now he was ill, and it was reported that he could not live. A new Emperor had already been chosen, and the people stood in the street, outside the palace, and asked the Cavalier how the Emperor was?

"Pish!" said he, and shook his head.

Cold and pale lay the Emperor in his magnificent bed; all the court believed him to be already dead, and every one had hastened away to greet the new Emperor; the men ran out for a little gossip on the subject, and the maids were having a grand coffee-party.

The floors of all the rooms and passages were covered with cloth, in order that not a step should be heard—it was everywhere so still! so still! But the Emperor was not yet dead; stiff and pale he lay in his splendid bed, with the long velvet curtains, and heavy gold tassels. A window was opened above, and the moon shone down on the Emperor and the artificial bird.

The poor Emperor could scarcely breathe; it appeared to him as though something was sitting on his chest; he opened his eyes, and saw that it was Death, who had put on the Emperor's crown, and with one hand held the golden scimitar, with the other the splendid imperial banner; whilst, from under the folds of the thick velvet hangings, the strangest-looking heads were seen peering forth; some with an expression absolutely hideous, and others with an extremely gentle and lovely aspect: they were the bad and good deeds of the Emperor, which were now all fixing their eyes upon him, whilst Death sat on his heart.

"Dost thou know this?" they whispered one after another. "Dost thou remember that?" And they began reproaching him in such a manner that the sweat broke out upon his forehead.

"I have never known anything like it," said the Emperor. "Music, music, the great Chinese drum!" cried he; "let me not hear what they are saying."

They went on, however; and Death, quite in the Chinese fashion, nodded his head to every word.

"Music, music!" cried the Emperor. "Thou dear little artificial bird! sing, I pray thee, sing!—I have given thee gold and precious stones, I have even hung my golden slippers round thy neck— sing, I pray thee, sing!"

But the bird was silent; there was no one there to wind him up, and he could not sing without this. Death continued to stare at the Emperor with his great hollow eyes! and everywhere it was still, fearfully still!

All at once the sweetest song was heard from the window; it was the little living nightingale who was sitting on a branch outside—she had heard of her Emperor's severe illness, and was come to sing to him of comfort and hope. As she sang, the spectral forms became paler and paler, the blood flowed more and more quickly through the Emperor's feeble members, and even Death listened and said, "Go on, little nightingale, go on."

"Wilt thou give me the splendid gold scimitar? Wilt thou give me the gay banner, and the Emperor's crown?"

And Death gave up all these treasures for a song; and the nightingale sang on: she sang of the quiet churchyard, where white roses blossom, where the lilac sends forth its fragrance, and the fresh grass is bedewed with the tears of the sorrowing friends of the departed. Then Death was seized with a longing after his garden, and like a cold white shadow, flew out at the window.

"Thanks, thanks," said the Emperor, "thou heavenly little bird, I know thee well. I have banished thee from my realm, and thou hast sung away those evil faces from my bed, and Death from my heart; how shall I reward thee?"

"Thou hast already rewarded me," said the nightingale; "I have seen tears in thine eyes, as when I sang to thee for the first time: those I shall never forget, they are jewels which do so much good to a minstrel's heart! but sleep now, and wake fresh and healthy; I will sing thee to sleep."

And she sang—and the Emperor fell into a sweet sleep. Oh, how soft and kindly was that sleep!

The sun shone in at the window when he awoke, strong and healthy. Not one of his servants had returned, for they all believed him dead; but the nightingale still sat and sang.

"Thou shalt always stay with me," said the Emperor, "thou shalt only sing when it pleases thee, and the artificial bird I will break into a thousand pieces."

"Do not so," said the nightingale; "truly he has done what he could; take care of him. I cannot stay in the palace; but let me come when I like: I will sit on the branches close to the window, in the evening, and sing to thee, that thou mayest become happy and thoughtful. I will sing to thee of the joyful and the sorrowing, I will sing to thee of all that is good or bad, which is concealed from thee. The little minstrel flies afar to the fisherman's hut, to the peasant's cottage, to all who are far distant from thee and thy court. I love thy heart more than thy crown, and yet the crown has an odor of something holy about it. I will come, I will sing. But thou must promise me one thing."

"Everything," said the Emperor. And now he stood in his imperial splendor, which he had put on himself, and held the scimitar so heavy with gold to his heart. "One thing I beg of thee: let no one know that thou hast a little bird, who tells thee everything, then all will go on well." And the nightingale flew away.

The attendants came in to look at their dead Emperor. Lo! there they stood—and the Emperor said, "Good-morning!"

THE · WILD · SWANS

THE WILD SWANS

FAR HENCE, IN A COUNTRY WHITHER THE SWALLOWS FLY IN OUR winter-time, there dwelt a King who had eleven sons, and one daughter, the beautiful Elise. The eleven brothers (they were princes) went to school with stars on their breasts and swords by their sides; they wrote on golden tablets with diamond pens, and could read either with a book or without one—in short, it was easy to perceive that they were princes. Their sister Elise used to sit upon a little glass stool, and had a picture-book which had cost the half of a kingdom. Oh, the children were so happy! but happy they were not to remain always.

Their father the King married a very wicked Queen, who was not at all kind to the poor children; they found this out on the first day after the marriage, when there was a grand gala at the palace; for when the children played at receiving company, instead of having as many cakes and sweetmeats as they liked, the Queen gave them only some sand in a little dish, and told them to imagine that was something nice.

The week after, she sent the little Elise to be brought up by some peasants in the country, and it was not long before she told the King so many falsehoods about the poor princes that he would have nothing more to do with them.

"Away, out into the world, and take care of yourselves," said the wicked Queen; "fly away in the form of great speechless birds." But she could not make their transformation so disagreeable as she wished,—the Princes were changed into eleven white swans. Sending forth a strange cry, they flew out of the palace windows, over the park and over the wood.

It was still early in the morning when they passed by the place where Elise lay sleeping in the peasant's cottage; they flew several times round the roof, stretched their long necks, and flapped their wings, but no one either heard or saw them; they were forced to fly away, up to the clouds and into the wide world, so on they went to the forest, which extended as far as the sea-shore.

The poor little Elise stood in the peasant's cottage amusing herself with a green leaf, for she had no other plaything. She pricked a hole in the leaf and peeped through it at the sun, and then she fancied she saw her brother's bright eyes, and whenever the warm sunbeams shone full upon her cheeks, she thought of her brother's kisses.

One day passed exactly like the other. When the wind blew through the thick hedge of rose-trees in front of the house, she would whisper to the roses, "Who is more beautiful than you?" but the roses would shake their heads and say, "Elise." And when the peasant's wife sat on Sundays at the door of her cottage reading her hymn-book, the wind would rustle in the leaves and say to the book, "Who is more pious than thou?"—"Elise," replied the hymn-book. And what the roses and the hymn-book said, was no more than the truth.

PLATE II.
The peasant's wife sat on Sundays at the door of
her cottage reading her hymn-book

Elise was now fifteen years old, she was sent for home; but when the Queen saw how beautiful she was, she hated her the more, and would willingly have transformed her like her brothers into a wild swan, but she dared not do so, because the King wished to see his daughter.

So the next morning the Queen went into a bath which was made of marble, and fitted up with soft pillows and the gayest carpets; she took three toads, kissed them, and said to one, "Settle thou upon Elise's head that she may become dull and sleepy like thee."—"Settle thou upon her forehead," said she to another, "and let her become ugly like thee, so that her father may not know her again." And "Do thou place thyself upon her bosom," whispered she to the third, "that her heart may become corrupt and evil, a torment to herself." She then put the toads into the clear water, which was immediately tinted with a green color, and having called Elise, took off her clothes and made her get into the bath—one toad settled among her hair, another on her forehead, and the third upon her bosom, but Elise seemed not at all aware of it; she rose up and three poppies were seen swimming on the water. Had not the animals been poisonous and kissed by a witch, they would have been changed into roses whilst they remained on Elise's head and heart—she was too good for magic to have any power over her. When the Queen perceived this, she rubbed walnut juice all over the maiden's skin, so that it became quite swarthy, smeared a nasty salve over her lovely face, and entangled her long thick hair,—it was impossible to recognize the beautiful Elise after this.

When her father saw her he was shocked, and said she could not be his daughter; no one would have anything to do with her

So Elise took off her clothes and stepped into the water

but the mastiff and the swallows; but they, poor things, could not say anything in her favor.

Poor Elise wept, and thought of her eleven brothers, not one of whom she saw at the palace. In great distress she stole away and wandered the whole day over fields and moors, till she reached the forest. She knew not where to go, but she was so sad, and longed so much to see her brothers, who had been driven out into the world, that she determined to seek and find them.

She had not been long in the forest when night came on, and she lost her way amid the darkness. So she lay down on the soft moss, said her evening prayer, and leaned her head against the trunk of a tree. It was so still in the forest, the air was mild, and from the grass and mold around gleamed the green light of many hundred glowworms, and when Elise lightly touched one of the branches hanging over her, bright insects fell down upon her like falling stars.

All the night long she dreamed of her brothers. They were all children again, played together, wrote with diamond pens upon golden tablets, and looked at the pictures in the beautiful book which had cost half of a kingdom. But they did not as formerly make straight strokes and pothooks upon the tablets; no, they wrote of the bold actions they had performed, and the strange adventures they had encountered, and in the picture-book everything seemed alive—the birds sang, men and women stepped from the book and talked to Elise and her brothers; however, when she turned over the leaves, they jumped back into their places, so that the pictures did not get confused together.

When Elise awoke the sun was already high in the heavens. She could not see it certainly, for the tall trees of the forest entwined their thickly leaved branches closely together, which, as the sunbeams played upon them, looked like a golden veil waving to and fro. And the air was so fragrant, and the birds perched upon Elise's shoulders. She heard the noise of water, there were several springs forming a pool, with the prettiest pebbles at the bottom, bushes were growing thickly round, but the deer had trodden a broad path through them, and by this path Elise went down to the water's edge. The water was so clear that had not the boughs and bushes around been moved to and fro by the wind, you might have fancied they were painted upon the smooth surface, so distinctly was each little leaf mirrored upon it, whether glowing in the sunlight or lying in the shade.

As soon as Elise saw her face reflected in the water, she was quite startled, so brown and ugly did it look; however, when she wetted her little hand, and rubbed her brow and eyes, the white skin again appeared.—So Elise took off her clothes, stepped into the fresh water, and in the whole world there was not a king's daughter more beautiful than she then appeared.

After she had again dressed herself, and had braided her long hair, she went to the bubbling spring, drank out of the hollow of her hand, and then wandered farther into the forest. She knew not where she was going, but she thought of her brothers, and of the good God who, she felt, would never forsake her. He it was who made the wild crab-trees grow in order to feed the hungry, and who showed her a tree whose boughs bent under the weight of their fruit. She made her noonday meal under its shade, propped up the boughs, and then walked on amid the dark twilight of the forest. It was so still that she could hear her own footsteps, and the rustling of each little withered leaf that was crushed beneath her feet; not a bird was to be seen, not a single sunbeam penetrated through the thick foliage, and the tall stems of the trees stood so close together, that when she looked straight before her, she seemed enclosed by trellis-work upon trellis-work. Oh! there was a solitariness in this forest such as Elise had never known before.

And the night was so dark! not a single glowworm sent forth its light. Sad and melancholy she lay down to sleep, and then it seemed to her as though the boughs above her opened, and that she saw the Angel of God looking down upon her with gentle aspect, and a thousand little cherubs all around him. When she awoke in the morning she could not tell whether this was a dream, or whether she had really been so watched.

She walked on a little farther and met an old woman with a basket full of berries; the old woman gave her some of them, and Elise asked if she had not seen eleven princes ride through the wood.

"No," said the old woman, "but I saw yesterday eleven Swans with golden crowns on their heads swim down the brook near this place."

And she led Elise on a little farther to a precipice, the base of which was washed by a brook; the trees on each side stretched their long leafy branches towards each other, and where they could not unite, the roots had disengaged themselves from the earth and hung their interlaced fibers over the water.

Elise bade the old woman farewell, and wandered by the side of the stream till she came to the place where it reached the open sea.

The great, the beautiful sea lay extended before the maiden's eyes, but not a ship, not a boat was to be seen; how was she to

And met an old woman with a basket full of berries

go on? She observed the numberless little stones on the shore, all of which the waves had washed into a round form; glass, iron, stone, everything that lay scattered there, had been molded into shape, and yet the water which had effected this was much softer than Elise's delicate little hand. "It rolls on unweariedly," said she, "and subdues what is so hard; I will be no less unwearied! Thank you for the lesson you have given me, ye bright rolling waves; some day, my heart tells me, you shall carry me to my dear brothers!"

There lay upon the wet sea-grass eleven white swan feathers; Elise collected them together; drops of water hung about them, whether dew or tears she could not tell. She was quite alone on

Not a boat was to be seen

the sea-shore, but she did not care for that; the sea presented an eternal variety to her, more indeed in a few hours than the gentle inland waters would have offered in a whole year. When a black cloud passed over the sky, it seemed as if the sea would say, "I too can look dark," and then the wind would blow and the waves fling out their white foam; but when the clouds shone with a bright red tint, and the winds were asleep, the sea also became like a rose-leaf in hue; it was now green, now white, but as it reposed peacefully, a slight breeze on the shore caused the water to heave gently like the bosom of a sleeping child.

At sunset Elise saw eleven Wild Swans with golden crowns on their heads fly towards the land; they flew one behind another, looking like a streaming white ribbon. Elise climbed the precipice, and concealed herself behind a bush; the swans settled close to her, and flapped their long white wings.

As the sun sank beneath the water, the swans also vanished, and in their place stood eleven handsome princes, the brothers of Elise. She uttered a loud cry, for although they were very much altered, Elise knew that they were, felt that they must be, her brothers; she ran into their arms, called them by their names— and how happy were *they* to see and recognize their sister, who was now grown so tall and so beautiful! They laughed and wept, and soon told each other how wickedly their step-mother had acted towards them.

"We," said the eldest of the brothers, "fly or swim as long as the sun is above the horizon, but when it sinks below, we appear again in our human form; we are therefore obliged to look out for a safe resting-place, for if at sunset we were flying among the clouds, we should fall down as soon as we resumed our own form. We do not dwell here, a land quite as beautiful as this lies on the opposite side of the sea, but it is far off. To reach it, we have to cross the deep waters, and there is no island midway on which we may rest at night; one little solitary rock rises from the waves, and upon it we only just find room enough to stand side by side. There we spend the night in our human form, and when the sea is rough, we are sprinkled by its foam; but we are thankful for this resting-place, for without it we should never be able to visit our dear native country. Only once in the year is this visit to the home of our fathers permitted; we require two of the longest days for our flight, and can remain here only eleven days, during which time we fly over the large forest, whence we can see the palace in which we were born, where our father dwells, and the tower of the church in which our mother was buried. Here even the trees and bushes seem of kin to us, here the wild horses still race over the plains, as in the days of our childhood, here the charcoal-burner still sings the same old tunes to which we used to dance in our youth, here we are still attracted, and here we have found thee, thou dear little sister! We have yet two days longer to stay here, then we must fly over the sea to a land beautiful indeed, but not our fatherland. How shall we take thee with us? we have neither ship nor boat!"

"How shall I be able to release you?" said the sister. And so they went on talking almost the whole of the night. They slumbered only a few hours.

Elise was awakened by the rustling of swans' wings which were fluttering above her. Her brothers were again transformed, and for some time flew around in large circles. At last they flew far, far away; one of them remained behind, it was the youngest; he laid his head in her lap and she stroked his white wings; they remained the whole day together. Towards evening the others came back, and when the sun was set, again they stood on the firm ground in their natural form.

"To-morrow we shall fly away, and may not return for a year, but we cannot leave thee; hast thou courage to accompany us? My arm is strong enough to bear thee through the forest; shall we not have sufficient strength in our wings to transport thee over the sea?"

"Yes, take me with you," said Elise. They spent the whole night in weaving a mat of the pliant willow bark and the tough rushes, and their mat was thick and strong. Elise lay down upon it, and when the sun had risen, and the brothers were again transformed into wild swans, they seized the mat with their beaks and flew up high among the clouds with their dear sister, who was still sleeping. The sunbeams shone full upon her face, so one of the swans flew over her head, and shaded her with his broad wings.

They were already far from land when Elise awoke: she thought she was still dreaming, so strange did it appear to her to be travelling through the air, and over the sea. By her side lay a cluster of pretty berries, and a handful of savory roots. Her youngest brother had collected and laid them there; and she thanked him with a smile, for she knew him as the swan who flew over her head and shaded her with his wings.

They flew so high, that the first ship they saw beneath them seemed like a white sea-gull hovering over the water. Elise saw behind her a large cloud, it looked like a mountain, and on it she saw the gigantic shadows of herself and the eleven swans—it formed a picture more splendid than any she had ever yet seen; soon, however, the sun rose higher, the cloud remained far behind, and then the floating shadowy picture disappeared.

The whole day they continued flying with a whizzing noise somewhat like an arrow, but yet they went slower than usual— they had their sister to carry. A heavy tempest was gathering, the evening approached; anxiously did Elise watch the sun, it was setting. Still the solitary rock could not be seen; it appeared to her that the swans plied their wings with increasing vigor. Alas! it would be her fault if her brothers did not arrive at the place in time; they would become human beings when the sun set, and if this happened before they reached the rock, they must fall into the sea, and be drowned. She prayed to God most fervently, still no rock was to be seen; the black clouds drew nearer, violent gusts of wind announced the approach of a tempest, the clouds rested perpendicularly upon a fearfully large wave which rolled quickly forwards, one flash of lightning rapidly succeeded another.

The sun was now on the rim of the sea. Elise's heart beat violently; the swans shot downwards so swiftly that she thought she must fall, but again they began to hover; the sun was half sunk beneath the water, and at that moment she saw the little rock below her; it looked like a seal's head when he raises it just

There was only just room for
her and them

above the water. And the sun was sinking fast,—it seemed scarcely larger than a star,—her foot touched the hard ground, and it vanished altogether, like the last spark on a burnt piece of paper. Arm in arm stood her brothers around her—there was only just room for her and them; the sea beat tempestuously against the rock, flinging over them a shower of foam; the sky seemed in a continual blaze, with the fast-succeeding flashes of fire that lightened it, and peal after peal rolled on the thunder, but sister and brothers kept firm hold of each other's hands. They sang a psalm, and their psalm gave them comfort and courage.

By daybreak the air was pure and still, and as soon as the sun rose, the swans flew away with Elise from the rock. The waves rose higher and higher, and when they looked from the clouds down upon the blackish-green sea, covered as it was with white foam, they might have fancied that millions of swans were swimming on its surface.

As day advanced, Elise saw floating in the air before her a land of mountains intermixed with glaciers, and in the center a palace a mile in length, with splendid colonnades, surrounded by palm-trees and gorgeous-looking flowers as large as mill wheels. She asked if this were the country to which they were flying, but the swans shook their heads, for what she saw was the beautiful airy castle of the fairy Morgana, where no human being was admitted; and whilst Elise still bent her eyes upon it, mountains, trees, and castle all disappeared, and in their place stood twelve churches with high towers and pointed windows—she fancied she heard the organ play, but it was only the murmur of the sea. She was now close to these churches, but behold! they have changed into a large fleet sailing under them; she looked down and saw it was only a sea-mist passing rapidly over the water. An eternal variety floated before her eyes, till at last the actual land to which she was going appeared in sight. Beautiful blue mountains, cedar woods, towns, and castles rose to view. Long before sunset Elise sat down among the mountains, in front of a large cavern; delicate young creepers grew around so thickly, that it appeared covered with gay embroidered carpets.

"Now we shall see what thou wilt dream of to-night!" said her youngest brother, as he showed her the sleeping-chamber destined for her.

"Oh that I could dream how you might be released from the spell!" said she; and this thought completely occupied her. She prayed most earnestly for God's assistance, nay, even in her dreams she continued praying, and it appeared to her that she was flying up high in the air towards the castle of the fairy Morgana. The fairy came forward to meet her, radiant and beautiful, and yet she fancied she resembled the old woman who had given her berries in the forest, and told her of the swans with golden crowns.

"Thou *canst* release thy brothers," said she, "but hast thou courage and patience sufficient? The water is indeed softer than thy delicate hands, and yet can mold the hard stones to its will, but then it cannot feel the pain which thy tender fingers will feel; it has no heart, and cannot suffer the anxiety and grief which thou must suffer. Dost thou see these stinging-nettles which I have in my hand? There are many of the same kind growing round the cave where thou art sleeping; only those that grow there or on the graves in the church-yard are of use, remember that! Thou must pluck them, although they will sting thy hand; thou must trample on the nettles with thy feet, and get yarn from them, and with this yarn thou must weave eleven shirts with long sleeves;—throw them over the eleven wild swans, and the spell is broken. But mark this: from the moment that thou beginnest thy work till it is completed, even should it occupy thee for years, thou must not speak a word; the first syllable that escapes thy lips will fall like a dagger into the hearts of thy brothers; on thy tongue depends their life. Mark well all this!"

And at the same moment the fairy touched Elise's hands with a nettle, which made them burn like fire, and Elise awoke. It was broad daylight, and close to her lay a nettle like the one she had seen in her dream. She fell upon her knees, thanked God, and then went out of the cave in order to begin her work. She plucked with her own delicate hands the disagreeable stinging-nettles; they burned large blisters on her hands and arms, but she bore the pain willingly in the hope of releasing her dear brothers. She trampled on the nettles with her naked feet, and spun the green yarn.

At sunset came her brothers. Elise's silence quite frightened them, they thought it must be the effect of some fresh spell of their wicked step-mother; but when they saw her blistered hands, they found out what their sister was doing for their sakes. The youngest brother wept, and when his tears fell upon her hands, Elise felt no more pain, the blisters disappeared.

The whole night she spent in her work, for she could not rest till she had released her brothers. All the following days she sat in her solitude, for the swans had flown away; but never had time passed so quickly. One shirt was ready; she now began the second.

Suddenly a hunting-horn resounded among the mountains. Elise was frightened. The noise came nearer, she heard the hounds barking; in great terror she fled into the cave, bound up the nettles which she had gathered and combed into a bundle, and sat down upon it.

In the same moment a large dog sprang out from the bushes; two others immediately followed; they barked loudly, ran away and then returned. It was not long before the hunters stood in front of the cave; the handsomest among them was the King of that country; he stepped up to Elise. Never had he seen a lovelier maiden.

"How earnest thou here, thou beautiful child?" said he. Elise shook her head; she dared not speak, a word might have cost her the life of her brothers; and she hid her hands under her apron lest the King should see how she was suffering.

"Come with me," said he, "thou must not stay here! If thou art good as thou art beautiful, I will dress thee in velvet and silk, I will put a gold crown upon thy head, and thou shalt dwell in my palace!" So he lifted her upon his horse, while she wept and wrung her hands; but the King said, "I only desire thy happiness! thou shalt thank me for this some day!" and away he rode over mountains and valleys, holding her on his horse in front, whilst the other hunters followed. When the sun set, the King's magnificent capital with its churches and cupolas lay before them, and the King led Elise into the palace, where, in a high marble hall, fountains were playing, and the walls and ceiling displayed the most beautiful paintings. But Elise cared not for all this splendor; she wept and mourned in silence, even whilst some female attendants dressed her in royal robes, wove costly pearls in her hair, and drew soft gloves over her blistered hands.

And now she was full dressed, and as she stood in her splendid attire, her beauty was so dazzling, that the courtiers all bowed low before her; and the King chose her for his bride, although the Archbishop shook his head, and whispered that the "beautiful lady of the wood must certainly be a witch, who had blinded their eyes, and infatuated the King's heart."

But the King did not listen; he ordered that music should be played. A sumptuous banquet was served up, and the loveliest maidens danced round the bride; she was led through fragrant gardens into magnificent halls, but not a smile was seen to play upon her lips or beam from her eyes. The King then opened a small room next her sleeping apartment; it was adorned with costly green tapestry, and exactly resembled the cave in which she had been found; upon the ground lay the bundle of yarn which she had spun from the nettles, and by the wall hung the shirt she had completed. One of the hunters had brought all this, thinking there must be something wonderful in it.

"Here thou mayest dream of thy former home," said the King; "here is the work which employed thee; amidst all thy present splendor it may sometimes give thee pleasure to fancy thyself there again."

When Elise saw what was so dear to her heart, she smiled, and the blood returned to her cheeks; she thought her brothers might still be released, and she kissed the King's hand; he pressed her to his heart and ordered the bells of all the churches in the city to be rung, to announce the celebration of their wedding. The beautiful dumb maiden of the wood was to become Queen of the land.

The Archbishop whispered evil words in the King's ear, but they made no impression upon him; the marriage was solemnized, and the Archbishop himself was obliged to put the crown upon her head. In his rage he pressed the narrow rim so firmly on her forehead that it hurt her; but a heavier weight (sorrow for her brothers) lay upon her heart, she did not feel bodily pain. She was still silent, a single word would have killed her brothers; her eyes, however, beamed with heartfelt love to the King, so good and handsome, who had done so much to make her happy. She became more warmly attached to him every day. Oh, how much she wished she might confide to him all her sorrows! but she was forced to remain silent, she could not speak until her work was completed. To this end she stole away every night, and went into the little room that was fitted up in imitation of the cave; there she worked at her shirts, but by the time she had begun the seventh all her yarn was spent.

She knew that the nettles she needed grew in the church-yard, but she must gather them herself; how was she to get them?

"Oh, what is the pain in my fingers compared to the anguish my heart suffers?" thought she. "I must venture to the church-yard; the good God will not withdraw His protection from me!"

Fearful as though she were about to do something wrong, one moonlight night she crept down to the garden, and through the long avenues got into the lonely road leading to the church-yard. She saw sitting on one of the broadest tombstones a number of ugly old witches. They took off their ragged clothes as if they were going to bathe, and digging with their long lean fingers into the fresh grass, drew up the dead bodies and devoured the flesh. Elise was obliged to pass close by them, and the witches fixed their wicked eyes upon her; but she repeated her prayer, gathered the stinging-nettles, and took them back with her into the palace. One person only had seen her; it was the Archbishop, he was awake when others slept; now he was convinced that all was not right about the Queen: she must be a witch, who had through her enchantments infatuated the King, and all the people.

In the Confessional he told the King what he had seen, and what he feared; and when the slanderous words came from his lips, the sculptured images of the saints shook their heads as though they would say, "It is untrue, Elise is innocent!"

But the Archbishop explained the omen quite otherwise; he thought it was a testimony against her that the holy images shook their heads at hearing of her sin.

Two large tears rolled down the King's cheeks. He returned home in doubt; he pretended to sleep at night, though sleep never visited him; and he noticed that Elise rose from her bed every night, and every time he followed her secretly and saw her enter her little room.

"I must venture to the church-yard"

His countenance became darker every day; Elise perceived it, though she knew not the cause. She was much pained, and besides, what did she not suffer in her heart for her brothers! Her bitter tears ran down on the royal velvet and purple; they looked like bright diamonds, and all who saw the magnificence that surrounded her, wished themselves in her place. She had now nearly finished her work, only one shirt was wanting; unfortunately, yarn was wanting also, she had not a single nettle left. Once more, only this one time, she must go to the church-yard and gather a few handfuls. She shuddered when she thought of the solitary walk and of the horrid witches, but her resolution was as firm as her trust in God.

Elise went; the King and the Archbishop followed her; they saw her disappear at the church-yard door, and when they came nearer, they saw the witches sitting on the tombstones as Elise had seen them, and the King turned away, for he believed her whose head had rested on his bosom that very evening to be amongst them. "Let the people judge her!" said he. And the people condemned her to be burnt.

She was now dragged from the King's sumptuous apartments into a dark, damp prison, where the wind whistled through the grated window. Instead of velvet and silk, they gave her the bundle of nettles she had gathered; on that must she lay her head, the shirts she had woven must serve her as mattress and counterpane;—but they could not have given her anything she valued so much; and she continued her work, at the same time praying earnestly to her God. The boys sang scandalous songs about her in front of her prison; not a soul comforted her with one word of love.

Towards evening she heard the rustling of Swans' wings at the grating. It was the youngest of her brothers, who had at last found his sister, and she sobbed aloud for joy, although she knew that the coming night would probably be the last of her life; but then her work was almost finished and her brother was near.

The Archbishop came in order to spend the last hour with her; he had promised the King he would; but she shook her head and entreated him with her eyes and gestures to go—this night she must finish her work, or all she had suffered, her pain, her anxiety, her sleepless nights, would be in vain. The Archbishop went away with many angry words, but the unfortunate Elise knew herself to be perfectly innocent, and went on with her work.

Little mice ran busily about and dragged the nettles to her feet, wishing to help her; and the thrush perched on the iron bars of the window, and sang all night as merrily as he could, that Elise might not lose courage.

It was still twilight, just one hour before sunrise, when the eleven brothers stood before the palace gates, requesting an audience with the King; but it could not be, they were told, it was still night, the King was asleep, and they dared not wake him. They entreated, they threatened, the guard came up, the King himself at last stepped out to ask what was the matter,—at that moment the sun rose, the brothers could be seen no longer, and eleven white Swans flew away over the palace.

The people poured forth from the gates of the city; they wished to see the witch burnt. One wretched horse drew the cart in which Elise was placed; a coarse frock of sackcloth had been put on her, her beautiful long hair hung loosely over her shoulders, her cheeks were of a deadly paleness, her lips moved gently, and her fingers wove the green yarn: even on her way to her cruel death she did not give up her work; the ten shirts lay at her feet, she was now laboring to complete the eleventh. The rabble insulted her.

"Look at the witch, how she mutters! She has not a hymn-book in her hand, no, there she sits with her accursed hocus-pocus. Tear it from her, tear it into a thousand pieces!"

And they all crowded about her, and were on the point of snatching away the shirts, when eleven white Swans came flying towards the cart; they settled all round her, and flapped their wings. The crowd gave way in terror.

"It is a sign from Heaven! she is certainly innocent!" whispered some; they dared not say so aloud.

The Sheriff now seized her by the hand—in a moment she threw the eleven shirts over the Swans, and eleven handsome Princes appeared in their place. The youngest had, however, only one arm, and a wing instead of the other, for one sleeve was deficient in his shirt, it had not been quite finished.

"Now I may speak," said she: "I am innocent!"

And the people who had seen what had happened bowed before her as before a saint. She, however, sank lifeless in her brothers' arms; suspense, fear, and grief had quite exhausted her.

"Yes, she is innocent," said her eldest brother, and he now related their wonderful history. Whilst he spoke a fragrance as delicious as though it proceeded from millions of roses, diffused itself around, for every piece of wood in the funeral pile had taken root and sent forth branches, a hedge of blooming red roses surrounded Elise, and above all the others blossomed a flower of dazzling white color, bright as a star; the King plucked it and laid it on Elise's bosom, whereupon she awoke from her trance with peace and joy in her heart.

And all the church-bells began to ring of their own accord, and birds flew to the spot in swarms, and there was a festive procession back to the palace, such as no King has ever seen equaled.

I have scarcely closed my eyes the whole night through

The Princess and the Pea

THERE WAS ONCE A PRINCE WHO WISHED TO MARRY A PRINCESS; but then she must be a real Princess. He travelled all over the world in hopes of finding such a lady; but there was always something wrong. Princesses he found in plenty; but whether they were real Princesses it was impossible for him to decide, for now one thing, now another, seemed to him not quite right about the ladies. At last he returned to his palace quite cast down, because he wished so much to have a real Princess for his wife.

One evening a fearful tempest arose; it thundered and lightened, and the rain poured down from the sky in torrents; besides, it was as dark as pitch. All at once there was heard a violent knocking at the door, and the old King, the Prince's father, went out himself to open it.

It was a Princess who was standing outside the door. What with the rain and the wind, she was in a sad condition: the water trickled down from her hair, and her clothes clung to her body. She said she was a real Princess.

"Ah, we shall soon see that!" thought the old Queen-mother; however, she said not a word of what she was going to do, but went quietly into the bedroom, took all the bedclothes off the

PLATE 12.
Princesses he found in plenty; but whether they were
real Princesses it was impossible for him to decide

bed, and put three little peas on the bedstead. She then laid twenty mattresses one upon another over the three peas, and put twenty feather-beds over the mattresses.

Upon this bed the Princess was to pass the night.

The next morning she was asked how she had slept. "Oh, very badly indeed!" she replied. "I have scarcely closed my eyes the whole night through. I do not know what was in my bed, but I had something hard under me, and am all over black and blue. It has hurt me so much!"

Now it was plain that the lady must be a real Princess, since she had been able to feel the three little peas through the twenty mattresses and twenty feather-beds. None but a real Princess could have had such a delicate sense of feeling.

The Prince accordingly made her his wife, being now convinced that he had found a real Princess. The three peas were, however, put into the cabinet of curiosities, where they are still to be seen, provided they are not lost.

Was not this a lady of real delicacy?

The three peas were, however, put into the cabinet of curiosities

Karen

T
HERE WAS ONCE A LITTLE GIRL, VERY PRETTY AND DELICATE,
but so poor that in summer-time she always went barefoot, and
in winter wore large wooden shoes, so that her little ankles
grew quite red and sore.

In the village dwelt the shoemaker's mother. She sat down
one day and made out of some old pieces of red cloth a pair of
little shoes; they were clumsy enough, certainly, but they fitted
the little girl tolerably well, and she gave them to her. The little
girl's name was Karen.

It was the day of her mother's funeral when the red shoes were
given to Karen; they were not at all suitable for mourning, but she
had no others, and in them she walked with bare legs behind the
miserable straw bier.

Just then a large old carriage rolled by; in it sat a large old
lady; she looked at the little girl and pitied her, and she said to the
priest, "Give me the little girl and I will take care of her."

And Karen thought it was all for the sake of the red shoes that
the old lady had taken this fancy to her, but the old lady said they
were frightful, and they were burnt. And Karen was dressed very
neatly; she was taught to read and to work; and people told her

PLATE 13.
She sat down one day and made out of some old pieces
of red cloth a pair of little shoes

she was pretty—but the mirror said, "Thou art more than pretty, thou art beautiful!"

It happened one day that the Queen travelled through that part of the country with her little daughter, the Princess; and all the people, Karen amongst them, crowded in front of the palace, whilst the little Princess stood, dressed in white, at a window, for every one to see her. She wore neither train nor gold crown; but on her feet were pretty red morocco shoes, much prettier ones indeed than those the shoemaker's mother had made for little Karen. Nothing in the world could be compared to these red shoes!

Karen was now old enough to be confirmed, she was to have both new frock and new shoes. The rich shoemaker in the town took the measure of her little foot. Large glass cases full of neat shoes and shining boots were fixed round the room; however, the old lady's sight was not very good, and, naturally enough, she had not so much pleasure in looking at them as Karen had. Amongst the shoes was a pair of red ones, just like those worn by the Princess. How gay they were! and the shoemaker said they had been made for a count's daughter, but had not quite fitted her.

"They are of polished leather," said the old lady, "see how they shine!"

"Yes, they shine beautifully!" exclaimed Karen. And as the shoes fitted her, they were bought; but the old lady did not know that they were red, for she would never have suffered Karen to go to confirmation in red shoes. But Karen did so. Everybody looked at her feet, and as she walked up the nave to the chancel, it seemed to her that even the antique sculptured figures on the monuments, with their stiff ruffs and long black robes, fixed their eyes on her red shoes. Of them only she thought when the Bishop

And Karen was dressed very neatly

laid his hand on her head, when he spoke of Holy Baptism, of
her covenant with God, and how that she must now be a full-
grown Christian. The organ sent forth its deep, solemn tones, the
children's sweet voices mingled with those of the choristers, but
Karen still thought only of her red shoes.

That afternoon, when the old lady was told that Karen had
worn red shoes at her confirmation, she was much vexed, and told

Karen that they were quite unsuitable, and that, henceforward, whenever she went to church, she must wear black shoes, were they ever so old.

Next Sunday was the communion day. Karen looked first at the red shoes, then at the black ones, then at the red again, and— put them on.

It was beautiful sunshiny weather; Karen and the old lady walked to church through the corn-fields; the path was very dusty.

At the church door stood an old soldier; he was leaning on crutches, and had a marvelously long beard, not white, but reddish-hued, and he bowed almost to the earth, and asked the old lady if he might wipe the dust off her shoes. And Karen put out her little foot also. "Oh, what pretty dancing-shoes!" quoth the old soldier; "take care, and mind you do not let them slip off when you dance"; and he passed his hands over them.

Karen and the old lady walked to church

The old lady gave the soldier a halfpenny, and then went with Karen into church.

And every one looked at Karen's red shoes; and all the carved figures, too, bent their gaze upon them; and when Karen knelt before the altar, the red shoes still floated before her eyes; she thought of them and of them only, and she forgot to join in the hymn of praise—she forgot to repeat "Our Father."

At last all the people came out of church, and the old lady got into her carriage. Karen was just lifting her foot to follow her, when the old soldier standing in the porch exclaimed, "Only look, what pretty dancing-shoes!" And Karen could not help it, she felt she must make a few of her dancing steps; and after she had once begun, her feet continued to move, just as though the shoes had received power over them; she danced round the church-yard, she could not stop. The coachman was obliged to run after her; he took hold of her and lifted her into the carriage, but the feet still continued to dance, so as to kick the good old lady most cruelly. At last the shoes were taken off, and the feet had rest.

And now the shoes were put away in a press, but Karen could not help going to look at them every now and then.

The old lady lay ill in bed; the doctor said she could not live much longer. She certainly needed careful nursing, and who should be her nurse and constant attendant but Karen? But there was to be a grand ball in the town. Karen was invited; she looked at the old lady who was almost dying—she looked at the red shoes—she put them on, there could be no harm in doing that, at least; she went to the ball, and began to dance. But when she wanted to move to the right, the shoes bore her to the left; and when she would dance up the room, the shoes danced down the room, danced down the stairs, through the streets, and through the gates of the town. Dance she did, and dance she must, straight out into the dark wood.

Something all at once shone through the trees. She thought at first it must be the moon's bright face, shining blood-red through the night mists; but no, it was the old soldier with the red beard—he sat there, nodding at her, and repeating, "Only look, what pretty dancing-shoes!"

She was very much frightened, and tried to throw off her red shoes, but could not unclasp them. She hastily tore off her stockings; but the shoes she could not get rid of—they had, it seemed, grown on to her feet. Dance she did, and dance she must, over field and meadow, in rain and in sunshine, by night and by day. By night! that was most horrible! She danced into the lonely church-yard, but the dead there danced not, they were at rest. She would fain

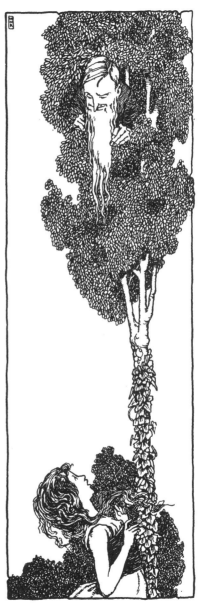

He sat there nodding at her

have sat down on the poor man's grave, where the bitter tansy grew, but for her there was neither rest nor respite. She danced past the open church door; there she saw an angel, clad in long white robes, and with wings that reached from his shoulders to the earth; his countenance was grave and stern, and in his hand he held a broad glittering sword.

"Dance thou shalt," said he; "dance on, in thy red shoes, till thou art pale and cold, and thy skin shrinks and crumples up like a skeleton's! Dance thou shalt still, from door to door, and wherever proud, vain children live thou shalt knock, so that they may hear thee and fear! Dance shalt thou, dance on—"

"Mercy!" cried Karen; but she heard not the angel's answer, for the shoes carried her through the gate, into the fields, along highways and by-ways, and still she must dance.

One morning she danced past a door she knew well; she heard psalm-singing from within, and presently a coffin, strewn with flowers, was borne out. Then Karen knew that the good old lady was dead, and she felt herself a thing forsaken by all mankind, and accursed by the Angel of God.

Dance she did, and dance she must, even through the dark night; the shoes bore her continually over thorns and briars, till her limbs were torn and bleeding. Away she danced over the heath to a little solitary house; she knew that the headsman dwelt there, and she tapped with her fingers against the panes, crying—

"Come out! come out!—I cannot come in to you, I am dancing."

And the headsman replied, "Surely thou knowest not who I am. I cut off the heads of wicked men, and my axe is very sharp and keen."

Dance she must, over field and meadow

"Cut not off my head!" said Karen; "for then I could not live to repent of my sin; but cut off my feet with the red shoes."

And then she confessed to him all her sin, and the headsman cut off her feet with the red shoes on them; but even after this the shoes still danced away with those little feet over the fields, and into the deep forests.

And the headsman made her a pair of wooden feet and hewed down some boughs to serve her as crutches, and he taught her the psalm which is always repeated by criminals, and she kissed the hand that had guided the axe, and went her way over the heath. "Now I have certainly suffered quite enough through the red shoes," thought Karen, "I will go to church and let people see me once more!" and she went as fast as she could to the church-porch, but as she approached it, the red shoes danced before her and she was frightened and turned her back.

All that week through she endured the keenest anguish and shed many bitter tears; however, when Sunday came, she said to herself, "Well, I must have suffered and striven enough by this time, I dare say I am quite as good as many of those who are holding their heads so high in church." So she took courage and went there, but she had not passed the church-yard gate before she saw the red shoes again dancing before her, and in great terror she again turned back, and more deeply than ever bewailed her sin.

She then went to the pastor's house, and begged that some employment might be given her, promising to work diligently and do all she could; she did not wish for any wages, she said, she only wanted a roof to shelter her, and to dwell with good people. And the pastor's wife had pity on her, and took her into her service. And Karen was grateful and industrious.

Every evening she sat silently listening to the pastor, while he read the Holy Scriptures aloud. All the children loved her, but when she heard them talk about dress and finery, and about being as beautiful as a queen, she would sorrowfully shake her head.

Again Sunday came, all the pastor's household went to church, and they asked her if she would not go too, but she sighed and looked with tears in her eyes upon her crutches.

When they were all gone, she went into her own little, lowly chamber—it was but just large enough to contain a bed and chair—and there she sat down with her psalm-book in her hand, and whilst she was meekly and devoutly reading in it, the wind wafted the tones of the organ from the church into her room, and she lifted up her face to heaven and prayed, with tears, "O God, help me!"

Then the sun shone brightly, so brightly!—and behold! close before her stood the white-robed Angel of God, the same whom she had seen on that night of horror at the church-porch, but his hand wielded not now, as then, a sharp, threatening sword— he held a lovely green bough, full of roses. With this he touched the ceiling, which immediately rose to a great height, a bright gold star spangling in the spot where the Angel's green bough had touched it. And he touched the walls, whereupon the room widened, and Karen saw the organ, the old monuments, and the congregation all sitting in their richly carved seats and singing from their psalm-books.

For the church had come home to the poor girl in her narrow chamber, or rather the chamber had grown, as it were, into the church; she sat with the rest of the pastor's household, and, when the psalm was ended, they looked up and nodded to her, saying, "Thou didst well to come, Karen!"

"This is mercy!" said she.

And the organ played again, and the children's voices in the choir mingled so sweetly and plaintively with it! The bright sunbeams streamed warmly through the windows upon Karen's seat; her heart was so full of sunshine, of peace and gladness, that it broke; her soul flew upon a sunbeam to her Father in heaven, where not a look of reproach awaited her, not a word was breathed of the red shoes.

Two rogues, calling themselves weavers, made their appearance

The Emperor's New Clothes

ANY YEARS AGO, THERE WAS AN EMPEROR, WHO WAS SO excessively fond of new clothes that he spent all his money in dress. He did not trouble himself in the least about his soldiers; nor did he care to go either to the theater or the chase, except for the opportunities then afforded him for displaying his new clothes. He had a different suit for each hour of the day; and as of any other king or emperor one is accustomed to say, "He is sitting in council," it was always said of him, "the Emperor is sitting in his wardrobe."

Time passed away merrily in the large town which was his capital; strangers arrived every day at the court. One day, two rogues, calling themselves weavers, made their appearance. They gave out that they knew how to weave stuffs of the most beautiful colors and elaborate patterns, the clothes manufactured from which should have the wonderful property of remaining invisible to every one who was unfit for the office he held, or who was extraordinarily simple in character.

"These must indeed be splendid clothes!" thought the Emperor. "Had I such a suit, I might, at once, find out what men in my realms are unfit for their office, and also be able to distinguish the wise from the foolish! This stuff must be woven for me immediately." And he caused large sums of money to be given to both the weavers, in order that they might begin their work directly.

So the two pretended weavers set up two looms, and affected to work very busily, though in reality they did nothing at all. They asked for the most delicate silk and the purest gold thread, put both into their own knapsacks, and then continued their pretended work at the empty looms until late at night.

"I should like to know how the weavers are getting on with my cloth," said the Emperor to himself, after some little time had elapsed; he was, however, rather embarrassed, when he remembered that a simpleton, or one unfit for his office, would be unable to see the manufacture. "To be sure," he thought, "he had nothing to risk in his own person; but yet, he would prefer sending somebody else, to bring him intelligence about the weavers, and their work, before he troubled himself in the affair." All the people throughout the city had heard of the wonderful property the cloth was to possess; and all were anxious to learn how wise, or how ignorant, their neighbors might prove to be.

"I will send my faithful old minister to the weavers," said the Emperor at last, after some deliberation, "he will be best able to see how the cloth looks; for he is a man of sense, and no one can be more suitable for his office than he is."

So the faithful old minister went into the hall, where the knaves were working with all their might at their empty looms. "What can be the meaning of this?" thought the old man, opening his eyes very wide. "I cannot discover the least bit of thread on the looms!" However, he did not express his thoughts aloud.

The impostors requested him very courteously to be so good as to come nearer their looms; and then asked him whether the design pleased him, and whether the colors were not very beautiful, at the same time pointing to the empty frames. The poor old minister looked and looked, he could not discover anything on the looms, for a very good reason, viz. there was nothing there. "What!" thought he again, "is it possible that I am a simpleton? I have never thought so myself; and no one must know it now if I am so. Can it be that I am unfit for my office? No, that must not be said either. I will never confess that I could not see the stuff."

"Well, Sir Minister," said one of the knaves, still pretending to work, "you do not say whether the stuff pleases you."

"Oh, it is excellent!" replied the old minister, looking at the loom through his spectacles. "This pattern, and the colors— yes, I will tell the Emperor with out delay how very beautiful I think them."

"We shall be much obliged to you," said the impostors, and then they named the different colors and described the pattern of the pretended stuff. The old minister listened attentively to their words, in order that he might repeat them to the Emperor; and then the knaves asked for more silk and gold, saying that it was necessary to complete what they had begun. However, they put all that was given them into their knapsacks, and continued to work with as much apparent diligence as before at their empty looms.

"Oh, it is excellent!"
replied the minister

The Emperor now sent another officer of his court to see how the men were getting on, and to ascertain whether the cloth would soon be ready. It was just the same with this gentleman as with the minister; he surveyed the looms on all sides, but could see nothing at all but the empty frames.

"Does not the stuff appear as beautiful to you as it did to my lord the minister?" asked the impostors of the Emperor's second ambassador; at the same time making the same gestures as before, and talking of the design and colors which were not there.

"I certainly am not stupid!" thought the messenger. "It must be that I am not fit for my good, profitable office! That is very odd; however, no one shall know anything about it." And accordingly he praised the stuff he could not see, and declared that he was delighted with both colors and patterns. "Indeed, please your Imperial Majesty," said he to his sovereign, when he returned, "the cloth which the weavers are preparing is extraordinarily magnificent."

The whole city was talking of the splendid cloth which the Emperor had ordered to be woven at his own expense.

And now the Emperor himself wished to see the costly manufacture whilst it was still on the loom. Accompanied by a select number of officers of the court, among whom were the two honest men who had already admired the cloth, he went to the crafty impostors, who, as soon as they were aware of the Emperor's approach, went on working more diligently than ever, although they still did not pass a single thread through the looms.

"Is not the work absolutely magnificent?" said the two officers of the Crown, already mentioned. "If your Majesty will only be pleased to look at it! what a splendid design! what glorious colors!" and, at the same time, they pointed to the empty frames;

for they imagined that every one else could see this exquisite piece of workmanship.

"How is this?" said the Emperor to himself, "I can see nothing! this is indeed a terrible affair! Am I a simpleton, or am I unfit to be an Emperor? that would be the worst thing that could happen. Oh! the cloth is charming," said he aloud. "It has my complete approbation." And he smiled most graciously, and looked closely at the empty looms; for on no account would he say that he could not see what two of the officers of his court had praised so much. All his retinue now strained their eyes, hoping to discover something on the looms, but they could see no more than the others; nevertheless, they all exclaimed, "Oh, how beautiful!" and advised his Majesty to have some new clothes made from this splendid material, for the approaching procession. "Magnificent! charming! excellent!" resounded on all sides; and every one was uncommonly gay. The Emperor shared in the general satisfaction; and presented the impostors with the riband of an order of knighthood, to be worn in their button-holes, and the title of "Gentlemen Weavers."

The rogues sat up the whole of the night before the day on which the procession was to take place, and had sixteen lights burning, so that every one might see how anxious they were to finish the Emperor's new suit. They pretended to roll the cloth off the looms; cut the air with their scissors; and sewed with needles without any thread in them. "See!" cried they at last, "the Emperor's new clothes are ready!"

And now the Emperor, with all the grandees of his court, came to the weavers; and the rogues raised their arms, as if in the act of holding something up, saying, "Here are your Majesty's trousers! here is the scarf! here is the mantle! The whole suit is as light as a cobweb; one might fancy one has nothing at all on, when dressed in it; that, however, is the great virtue of this delicate cloth."

"Yes, indeed!" said all the court-iers, although not one of them could see anything of this exquisite manufacture.

As if in the act of holding something up

"If your Imperial Majesty will be graciously pleased to take off your clothes, we will fit on the new suit in front of the looking-glass."

The Emperor was accordingly undressed, and the rogues pretended to array him in his new suit; the Emperor turning round, from side to side, before the looking-glass.

"How splendid his Majesty looks in his new clothes! and how well they fit!" every one cried out. "What a design! what colors! these are indeed royal robes!"

"The canopy which is to be borne over your Majesty in the procession is waiting," announced the chief master of the ceremonies.

"I am quite ready," answered the Emperor. "Do my new clothes fit well?" asked he, turning himself round again before the looking-glass, in order that he might appear to be examining his handsome suit.

The lords of the bed-chamber, who were to carry his Majesty's train, felt about on the ground, as if they were lifting up the ends of the mantle, and pretending to be carrying some thing; for they would by no means betray anything like simplicity or unfitness for their office.

So now the Emperor walked under his high canopy in the midst of the procession, through the streets of his capital; and all the people standing by, and those at the windows, cried out, "Oh! how beautiful are our Emperor's new clothes! what a magnificent train there is to the mantle! and how gracefully the scarf hangs!" in short, no one would allow that he could not see these much-admired clothes; because, in doing so, he would have declared himself either a simpleton or unfit for his office. Certainly, none of the Emperor's various suits had ever made so great an impression as these invisible ones.

"But the Emperor has nothing at all on!" said a little child. "Listen to the voice of innocence!" exclaimed his father; and what the child had said was whispered from one to another.

"But he has nothing at all on!" at last cried out all the people. The Emperor was vexed, for he knew that the people were right; but he thought the procession must go on now! And the lords of the bed-chamber took greater pains than ever to appear holding up a train, although, in reality, there was no train to hold.

So now the emperor walked under his high canopy

The emperor's daughter

THE SWINEHERD

HERE WAS ONCE A POOR PRINCE, WHO HAD A KINGDOM; HIS kingdom was very small, but still quite large enough to marry upon; and he wished to marry.

It was certainly rather cool of him to say to the Emperor's daughter, Will you have me? But so he did; for his name was renowned far and wide; and there were a hundred princesses who would have answered "Yes!" and "Thank you kindly." We shall see what this Princess said.

Listen!

It happened that where the Prince's father lay buried, there grew a rose-tree—a most beautiful rose-tree, which blossomed only once in every five years, and even then bore only one flower, but that *was* a rose! It smelt so sweet, that all cares and sorrows were forgotten by him who inhaled its fragrance.

And furthermore, the Prince had a nightingale, who could sing in such a manner that it seemed as though all sweet melodies dwelt in her little throat. So the Princess was to have the rose, and the nightingale; and they were accordingly put into large silver caskets, and sent to her.

The Emperor had them brought into a large hall, where the Princess was playing at "Visiting," with the ladies of the court; and when she saw the caskets with the presents, she clapped her hands for joy.

All cares and sorrows were forgotten by him who inhaled its fragrance

"Ah, if it were but a little pussy-cat!" said she—but the rose-tree with its beautiful rose came to view.

"Oh, how prettily it is made!" said all the court ladies.

"It is more than pretty," said the Emperor, "it is charming!"

But the Princess touched it, and was almost ready to cry.

"Fie, papa!" said she, "it is not made at all, it is natural!"

"Let us see what is in the other casket, before we get into a bad humor," said the Emperor. So the nightingale came forth, and sang so delightfully that at first no one could say anything ill-humored of her.

"*Superbe! charmant!*" exclaimed the ladies; for they all used to chatter French, each one worse than her neighbor.

"How much the bird reminds me of the musical box that belonged to our blessed Empress," said an old knight. "Oh yes! these are the same tones, the same execution."

"Yes! yes!" said the Emperor, and he wept like a child at the remembrance.

"I will still hope that it is not a real bird," said the Princess.

"Yes, it is a real bird," said those who had brought it. "Well, then, let the bird fly," said the Princess; and she positively refused to see the Prince.

And he wept like a child

However, he was not to be discouraged; he daubed his face over brown and black, pulled his cap over his ears, and knocked at the door.

"Good day to my lord the Emperor!" said he. "Can I have employment at the palace?"

"Why, yes," said the Emperor, "I want some one to take care of the pigs, for we have a great many of them."

So the Prince was appointed "Imperial Swineherd." He had a dirty little room close by the pig-sty; and there he sat the whole day, and worked. By the evening he had made a pretty little kitchen-pot. Little bells were hung all round it; and when the pot was boiling, these bells tinkled in the most charming manner, and played the old melody,

> "Ah! dear Augustine,
> All is gone, gone, gone!"

But what was still more curious, whoever held his finger in the smoke of the kitchen-pot, immediately smelt all the dishes that were cooking on every hearth in the city.—This, you see, was something quite different from the rose.

Now the Princess happened to walk that way; and when she heard the tune, she stood quite still, and seemed pleased; for she could play "Dear Augustine"; it was the only piece she knew; and she played it with one finger.

"Why, there is my piece," said the Princess; "that swineherd must certainly have been well educated! Go in and ask him the price of the instrument."

"Ah! Dear Augustine"

So one of the court ladies must run in; however, she drew on wooden slippers first.

"What will you take for the kitchen-pot?" said the lady.

"I will have ten kisses from the Princess," said the swineherd.

"Yes, indeed!" said the lady.

"I cannot sell it for less," rejoined the swineherd.

"He is an impudent fellow!" said the Princess, and she walked on; but when she had gone a little way, the bells tinkled so prettily,

> "Ah! dear Augustine,
> All is gone, gone, gone!"

"Stay," said the Princess. "Ask him if he will have ten kisses from the ladies of my court."

"No, thank you!" said the swineherd, "ten kisses from the Princess, or I keep the kitchen-pot myself."

"That must not be either!" said the Princess; "but do you all stand before me that no one may see us."

And the court-ladies placed themselves in front of her, and spread out their dresses: the swineherd got ten kisses, and the Princess—the kitchen-pot.

That was delightful! the pot was boiling the whole evening, and the whole of the following day. They knew perfectly well what was cooking at every fire throughout the city, from the chamberlain's to the cobbler's: the court ladies danced, and clapped their hands.

"We know who has soup, and who has pancakes for dinner to-day; who has cutlets, and who has eggs. How interesting!"

"Yes, but keep my secret, for I am an Emperor's daughter."

The swineherd—that is to say, the Prince, for no one knew that he was other than an ill-favored swineherd—let not a day pass without working at something; he at last constructed a rattle, which, when it was swung round, played all the waltzes and jig-tunes which have ever been heard since the creation of the world.

"Ah, that is *superbe*!" said the Princess when she passed by. "I have never heard prettier compositions! Go in and ask him the price of the instrument; but mind, he shall have no more kisses!"

"He will have a hundred kisses from the Princess!" said the lady who had been to ask.

"I think he is not in his right senses!" said the Princess, and walked on; but when she had gone a little way, she stopped again. "One must encourage art," said she. "I am the Emperor's daughter. Tell him he shall, as on yesterday, have ten kisses from me, and may take the rest from the ladies of the court."

"Oh!—but we should not like that at all!" said they. "What are you muttering?" asked the Princess; "if I can kiss him, surely you can! Remember that you owe every thing to me." So the ladies were obliged to go to him again.

"A hundred kisses from the Princess!" said he, "or else let every one keep his own."

"Stand round!" said she; and all the ladies stood round her whilst the kissing was going on.

"What can be the reason for such a crowd close by the pig-sty?" said the Emperor, who happened just then to step out on the balcony; he rubbed his eyes and put on his spectacles. "They are the ladies of the court; I must go down and see what they are about!" So he pulled up his slippers at the heel, for he had trodden them down.

As soon as he had got into the court-yard, he moved very softly, and the ladies were so much engrossed with counting the kisses that all might go on fairly, that they did not perceive the Emperor. He rose on his tiptoes.

PLATE 14.
The Swineherd scolded and the rain
poured down

"What is all this?" said he, when he saw what was going on, and he boxed the Princess's ears with his slipper, just as the swineherd was taking the eighty-sixth kiss.

"March out!" said the Emperor, for he was very angry; and both Princess and swineherd were thrust out of the city.

The Princess now stood and wept, the swineherd scolded, and the rain poured down.

"Alas! unhappy creature that I am!" said the Princess. "If I had but married the handsome young Prince! Ah, how unfortunate I am!"

And the swineherd went behind a tree, washed the black and brown color from his face, threw off his dirty clothes, and stepped forth in his princely robes; he looked so noble that the Princess could not help bowing before him.

"I am come to despise thee," said he. "Thou wouldst not have an honorable prince! thou couldst not prize the rose and the nightingale, but thou wast ready to kiss the swineherd for the sake of a trumpery plaything. Thou art rightly served."

He then went back to his own little kingdom, and shut the door of his palace in her face. Now she might well sing

> "Ah! dear Augustine,
>   All is gone, gone, gone!"

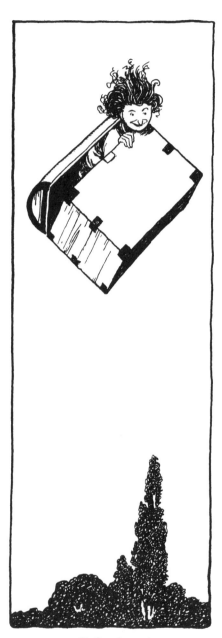

Up flew the trunk

THE FLYING TRUNK

THERE WAS ONCE A MERCHANT, SO RICH THAT HE MIGHT have paved the whole street where he lived and an alley besides with pieces of silver, but this he did not do; he knew another way of using his money, and whenever he laid out a shilling he gained a crown in return: a merchant he lived, and a merchant he died.

All his money then went to his son. But the son lived merrily and spent all his time in pleasures, went to masquerades every evening, made bank-notes into paper kites, and played at ducks and drakes in the pond with gold pieces instead of stones. In this manner his money soon vanished, until at last he had only a few pennies left, and his wardrobe was reduced to a pair of slippers and an old dressing-gown. His friends cared no more about him, now that they could no longer walk abroad with him; one of them, however, more good-natured than the rest, sent him an old trunk, with this advice, "Pack up, and be off!" This was all very fine, but he had nothing that he could pack up, so he put himself into the trunk.

It was a droll trunk! When the lock was pressed close it could fly. The merchant's son did press the lock, and lo! up flew the trunk with him through the chimney, high into the clouds, on and on, higher and higher; the lower part cracked, which rather frightened him, for if it had broken in two, a pretty fall he would have had!

However, it descended safely, and he found himself in Turkey. He hid the trunk under a heap of dry leaves in a wood, and walked into the next town: he could do so very well, for among the Turks everybody goes about clad as he was, in dressing-gown and slippers. He met a nurse, carrying a little child in her arms. "Hark ye, Turkish nurse," quoth he; "what palace is that with the high windows close by the town?"

The son lived merrily

"The King's daughter dwells there," replied the nurse; "it has been prophesied of her that she shall be made very unhappy by a lover, and therefore no one may visit her, except when the King and Queen are with her."

"Thank you," said the merchant's son, and he immediately went back into the wood, sat down in his trunk, flew up to the roof of the palace, and crept through the window into the Princess's apartment.

She was lying asleep on the sofa. She was so beautiful that the merchant's son could not help kneeling down to kiss her hand, whereupon she awoke, and was not a little frightened at the sight of this unexpected visitor; but he told her, however, that he was the Turkish prophet, and had come down from the sky on purpose to woo her, and on hearing this she was well pleased. So they sat down side by side, and he talked to her about her eyes, how that they were beautiful dark-blue seas, and that thoughts and feelings floated like mermaidens therein; and he spoke of her brow, how that it was a fair snowy mountain, with splendid halls and pictures, and many other such like things he told her.

Oh, these were charming stories! and thus he wooed the Princess, and she immediately said "Yes!"

"But you must come here on Saturday," said she; "the King and Queen have promised to drink tea with me that evening; they will be so proud and so pleased when they hear that I am to marry the Turkish prophet! And mind you tell them a very pretty story, for they are exceedingly fond of stories; my mother likes them to be very moral and aristocratic, and my father likes them to be merry, so as to make him laugh."

"Yes, I shall bring no other bridal present than a tale," replied the merchant's son; and here they parted, but not before the Princess had given her lover a sabre all covered with gold. He knew excellently well what use to make of this present.

So he flew away, bought a new dressing-gown, and then sat down in the wood to compose the tale which was to be ready by Saturday, and certainly he found composition not the easiest thing in the world.

At last he was ready, and at last Saturday came.

The King, the Queen, and the whole court were waiting tea for him at the Princess's palace. The suitor was received with much ceremony.

"Will you not tell us a story?"
asked the Queen

"Will you not tell us a story?" asked the Queen; "a story that is instructive and full of deep meaning."

"But let it make us laugh," said the King.

"With pleasure," replied the merchant's son; and now you must hear his story:—

There was once a bundle of matches, who were all extremely proud of their high descent, for their genealogical tree, that is to say, the tall fir-tree, from which each of them was a splinter, had been a tree of great antiquity, and distinguished by his height from all the other trees of the forest. The matches were now lying on the mantlepiece, between a tinder box and an old iron saucepan, and to these two they often talked about their youth. "Ah, when we were upon the green branches," said they; "when we really lived upon green branches—that was a happy time! Every morning and evening we had diamond-tea—that is, dew; the whole day long we had sunshine, at least whenever the sun shone, and all the little birds used to tell stories to us. It might easily be seen, too, that we were rich, for the other trees were clothed with leaves only during the summer, whereas our family could afford to wear green clothes both summer and winter. But at last came the wood-cutters: then was the great revolution, and our family was dispersed. The paternal trunk obtained a situation as mainmast to a magnificent ship, which could sail round the world if it chose; the boughs were transported to various places, and our vocation was henceforth to kindle lights for low, common people. Now you will understand how it comes to pass that persons of such high descent as we are should be living in a kitchen."

"To be sure, mine is a very different history," remarked the iron saucepan, near which the matches were lying. "From the moment I came into the world until now, I have been rubbed and scrubbed, and boiled over and over again—oh, how many times! I love to have to do with what is solidly good, and am really of the first importance in this house. My only recreation is to stand clean and bright upon this mantlepiece after dinner, and hold some rational conversation with my companions. However, excepting the water-pail, who now and then goes out into the court, we all of us lead a very quiet domestic life here. Our only newsmonger is the turf-basket, but he talks in such a democratic way about 'government' and the

"But let it make us laugh," said the King

'people'—why, I assure you, not long ago, there was an old jar standing here, who was so much shocked by what he heard said that he fell down from the mantlepiece and broke into a thousand pieces! That turf-basket is a Liberal, that's the fact."

"Now, you talk too much," interrupted the tinder-box, and the steel struck the flint, so that the sparks flew out. "Why should we not spend a pleasant evening?"

"Yes, let us settle who is of highest rank among us!" proposed the matches.

"Oh no; for my part I would rather not speak of myself," objected the earthenware pitcher. "Suppose we have an intellectual entertainment? I will begin; I will relate something of everyday life, such as we have all experienced; one can easily transport oneself into it, and that is so interesting! Near the Baltic, among the Danish beech-groves—"

"That is a capital beginning!" cried all the plates at once; "it will certainly be just the sort of story for me!"

"Yes, there I spent my youth in a very quiet family; the furniture was rubbed, the floors were washed, clean curtains were hung up every fortnight."

"How very interesting! what a charming way you have of describing things!" said the hair-broom. "Any one might guess immediately that it is a lady who is speaking; the tale breathes such a spirit of cleanliness!"

"Very true; so it does!" exclaimed the water-pail, and in the excess of his delight he gave a little jump, so that some of the water splashed upon the floor.

And the pitcher went on with her tale, and the end proved as good as the beginning.

All the plates clattered applause, and the hair-broom took some green parsley out of the sand-hole and crowned the pitcher, for he knew that this would vex the others; and, thought he, "If I crown her to-day, she will crown me to-morrow."

"Now I will dance," said the fire-tongs, and accordingly she did dance, and oh! it was wonderful to see how high she threw one of her legs up into the air; the old chair-cover in the corner tore with horror at seeing her. "Am not I to be crowned too?" asked the tongs, and she was crowned forthwith.

"These are the vulgar rabble!" thought the matches.

The tea-urn was now called upon to sing, but she had a cold; she said she could only sing when she was boiling; however, this was all her pride and affectation. The fact was she never cared to sing except when she was standing on the parlor-table before company.

On the window-ledge lay an old quill-pen, with which the maids used to write; there was nothing remarkable about her, except that she had been dipped too low in the ink; however, she was proud of that. "If the tea-urn does not choose to sing," quoth she, "she may let it alone; there is a nightingale in the cage hung just outside—he can sing; to be sure, he had never learnt the notes—never mind, we will not speak evil of any one this evening!"

"I think it highly indecorous," observed the tea-kettle, who was the vocalist of the kitchen, and a half-brother of the tea-urn's, "that a foreign bird should be listened to. Is it patriotic? I appeal to the turf-basket."

"I am only vexed," said the turf-basket. "I am vexed from my inmost soul that such things are thought of at all. Is it a becoming way of spending the evening? Would it not be much more rational to reform the whole house, and establish a totally new order of things, rather more according to nature? Then every one would get into his right place, and I would undertake to direct the revolution. What say you to it? That would be something worth the doing!"

"Oh yes, we will make a grand commotion!" cried they all. Just then the door opened—it was the servant-maid. They all stood perfectly still, not one dared stir, yet there was not a single kitchen utensil among them all but was thinking about the great things he could have done, and how great was his superiority over the others.

"Ah, if I had chosen it," thought each of them, "what a merry evening we might have had!"

The maid took the matches and struck a light—oh, how they sputtered and blazed up!

"Now every one may see," thought they, "that we are of highest rank; what a splendid, dazzling light we give, how glorious!"— and in another moment they were burnt out.

"That is a capital story," said the Queen; "I quite felt myself transported into the kitchen;—yes, thou shalt have our daughter!"

"With all my heart," said the King; "on Monday thou shalt marry our daughter." They said "thou" to him now, since he was so soon to become one of the family.

The wedding was a settled thing; and on the evening preceding, the whole city was illuminated; cakes, buns, and sugar-plums were thrown out among the people; all the little boys in the streets stood upon tiptoes, shouting "Hurrah!" and whistling through their fingers—it was famous!

"Well, I suppose I ought to do my part too," thought the merchant's son, so he went and bought sky-rockets, squibs, Catherine-wheels, Roman-candles, and all kinds of fireworks conceivable; put them all into his trunk, and flew up into the air, letting them off as he flew.

Hurrah! what a glorious sky-rocket was that!

Their slippers flew about their ears

All the Turks jumped up to look, so hastily that their slippers flew about their ears; such a meteor they had never seen before. Now they might be sure that it was indeed the prophet who was to marry their Princess.

As soon as the merchant's son had returned in his trunk to the wood, he said to himself, "I will now go into the city and hear what people say about me, and what sort of figure I made in the air." And, certainly, this was a very natural idea.

Oh, what strange accounts were given! Every one whom he accosted had beheld the bright vision in a way peculiar to himself, but all agreed that it was marvelously beautiful.

"I saw the great prophet with my own eyes," declared one; "he had eyes like sparkling stars, and a beard like foaming water."

"He flew enveloped in a mantle of fire," said another; "the prettiest little cherubs were peeping forth from under its folds."

Yes; he heard of many beautiful things, and the morrow was to be his wedding-day.

He now went back to the wood, intending to get into his trunk again, but where was it?

Alas! the trunk was burnt. One spark from the fireworks had been left in it, and set it on fire; the trunk now lay in ashes. The poor merchant's son could never fly again—could never again visit his bride.

She sat the livelong day upon the roof of her palace expecting him; she expects him still; he, meantime, goes about the world telling stories, but none of his stories now are so pleasant as that one which he related in the Princess's palace about the Brimstone Matches.

PLATE 15.
She sat the livelong day upon the roof of
her palace, expecting him

And thus the frog won the princess

THE LEAPING MATCH

T HE FLEA, THE GRASSHOPPER, AND THE FROG ONCE WANTED TO try which of them could jump highest; so they invited the whole world, and anybody else who liked, to come and see the grand sight. Three famous jumpers were they, as was seen by every one when they met together in the room.

"I will give my daughter to him who shall jump highest," said the King; "it would be too bad for you to have the trouble of jumping, and for us to offer you no prize."

The flea was the first to introduce himself; he had such polite manners, and bowed to the company on every side, for he was of noble blood; besides, he was accustomed to the society of man, which had been a great advantage to him.

Next came the grasshopper; he was not quite so slightly and elegantly formed as the flea; however, he knew perfectly well how to conduct himself, and wore a green uniform, which belonged to him by right of birth. Moreover, he declared himself to have sprung from a very ancient and honorable Egyptian family, and that in his present home he was very highly esteemed, so much so, indeed, that he had been taken out of the field and put into a card-house three stories high, built on purpose for him, and all of court-cards, the colored sides being turned inwards: as for the doors and windows in his house, they were cut out of the body of the Queen of Hearts. "And I can sing so well," added he, "that sixteen parlor-bred crickets, who have chirped and chirped ever since they were born and yet could never get anybody to build them a card-house, after hearing me have fretted themselves ten times thinner than ever, out of sheer envy and vexation!" Both the flea and the grasshopper knew excellently well how to make the most of themselves, and each considered himself quite an equal match for a princess.

The frog said not a word; however, it might be that he thought the more, and the house-dog, after going snuffing about him, confessed that the frog must be of a good family. And the old councilor, who in vain received three orders to hold his tongue, declared that the frog must be gifted with the spirit of prophecy, for that one could read on his back whether there was to be a severe or a mild winter, which, to be sure, is more than can be read on the back of the man who writes the weather almanac.

The old
councilor

"Ah, I say nothing for the present!" remarked the old King, "but I observe everything, and form my

"I say nothing for the present!" remarked the old King

own private opinion thereupon." And now the match began. The flea jumped so high that no one could see what had become of him, and so they insisted that he had not jumped at all, "which was disgraceful, after he had made such a fuss!"

The grasshopper only jumped half as high, but he jumped right into the King's face, and the King declared he was quite disgusted by his rudeness.

The frog stood still as if lost in thought; at last people fancied he did not intend to jump at all.

"I'm afraid he is ill!" said the dog; and he went snuffing at

It may not be perfectly true

him again, when lo! all at once he made a little side-long jump into the lap of the Princess, who was sitting on a low stool close by.

Then spoke the King: "There is nothing higher than my daughter, therefore he who jumps up to her jumps highest; but only a person of good understanding would ever have thought of that, and thus the frog has shown us that he has understanding. He has brains in his head, that he has!"

And thus the frog won the Princess.

"I jumped highest for all that!" exclaimed the flea. "But it's all the same to me; let her have the stiff-legged, slimy creature, if she like him! I jumped highest, but I am too light and airy for this stupid world; the people can neither see me nor catch me; dullness and heaviness win the day with them!"

And so the flea went into foreign service, where, it is said, he was killed.

And the grasshopper sat on a green bank, meditating on the world and its goings on, and at length he repeated the flea's last words—"Yes, dullness and heaviness win the day! dullness and heaviness win the day!" And then he again began singing his own peculiar, melancholy song, and it is from him that we have learnt this history; and yet, my friend, though you read it here in a printed book, it may not be perfectly true.

Her shoes and hat were gilt, her hand held a crook

The Shepherdess and the Chimney-Sweeper

AVE YOU NEVER SEEN AN OLD-FASHIONED OAKEN-WOOD cabinet, quite black with age and covered with varnish and carving work? Just such a piece of furniture, an old heir-loom that had been the property of its present mistress's great-grandmother, once stood in a parlor. It was carved from top to bottom—roses, tulips, and little stags' heads with long, branching antlers, peering forth from the curious scrolls and foliage surrounding them. Moreover, in the center panel of the cabinet was carved the full-length figure of a man, who seemed to be perpetually grinning, perhaps at himself, for in truth he was a most ridiculous figure; he had crooked legs, small horns on his forehead, and a long beard. The children of the house used to call him "the crooked-legged Field-marshal-Major-General Corporal-Sergeant," for this was a long, hard name, and not many figures, whether carved in wood or in stone, could boast of such a title. There he stood, his eyes always fixed upon the table under the pier-glass, for on this table stood a pretty little porcelain shepherdess, her mantle gathered gracefully round her, and fastened with a red rose; her shoes and hat were gilt, her hand held a crook—oh, she was charming! Close by her stood a little chimney-sweeper, likewise of porcelain.

He was as clean and neat as any of the other figures, indeed, the manufacturer might just as well have made a prince as a chimney-sweeper of him, for though elsewhere black as a coal, his face was as fresh and rosy as a girl's, which was certainly a mistake,—it ought to have been black. His ladder in his hand, there he kept his station, close by the little shepherdess; they had been placed together from the first, had always remained on the same spot, and had thus plighted their troth to each other; they suited each other so well, they were both young people, both of the same kind of porcelain, both alike fragile and delicate.

Not far off stood a figure three times as large as the others. It was an old Chinese mandarin who could nod his head; he too was of porcelain, and declared that he was grandfather to the little shepherdess. He could not prove his assertion; however, he insisted that he had authority over her, and so, when the crooked-legged Field-marshal-Major-General Corporal-Sergeant made proposals to the little shepherdess, he nodded his head in token of his consent.

"Now, you will have a husband," said the old mandarin to her, "a husband who, I verily believe, is of mahogany-wood; you will be the wife of a Field-marshal-Major-General-Corporal Sergeant,

Oh, she was charming!

of a man who has a whole cabinet full of silverplate, besides a store of no one knows what in the secret drawers!"

"I will not go into that dismal cabinet!" declared the little shepherdess. "I have heard say that eleven porcelain ladies are already imprisoned there."

"Then you shall be the twelfth, and you will be in good company!" rejoined the mandarin. "This very night, when the old cabinet creaks, your nuptials shall be celebrated, as sure as I am a Chinese mandarin!"

Whereupon he nodded his head and fell asleep.

But the little shepherdess wept, and turned to the beloved of her heart, the porcelain chimney-sweep.

"I believe I must ask you," said she, "to go out with me into the wide world, for here we cannot stay."

"I will do everything you wish," replied the little chimney-sweeper; "let us go at once. I think I can support you by my profession."

"If you could but get off the table!" sighed she; "I shall never be happy till we are away, out in the wide world."

And he comforted her, and showed her how to set her little foot on the carved edges and gilded foliage twining round the leg of the table, till at last they reached the floor. But turning to look at the old cabinet, they saw everything in a grand commotion, all the carved stags putting their little heads farther out, raising their antlers, and moving their throats, whilst "the crooked-legged Field-marshal-Major-General-Corporal-Sergeant" sprang up, and shouted out to the old Chinese mandarin, "Look, they are eloping! they are eloping!" They were not a little frightened, and quickly jumped into an open drawer for protection.

In this drawer there were three or four incomplete packs of cards, and also a little puppet-theatre; a play was being performed, and all the queens, whether of diamonds, hearts, clubs, or spades, sat in the front row fanning themselves with the flowers they held in their hands; behind them stood the knaves, showing that they had each two heads, one above and one below, as most cards have. The play was about two persons who were crossed in love, and the shepherdess wept over it, for it was just like her own history.

"I cannot bear this!" said she. "Let us leave the drawer." But when they had again reached the floor, on looking up at the table, they saw that the old Chinese mandarin had awakened, and was rocking his whole body to and fro with rage.

"Oh, the old mandarin is coming!" cried the little shepherdess, and down she fell on her porcelain knees in the greatest distress. "A sudden thought has struck me," said the chimney-sweeper: "suppose we creep into the large pot-pourri vase that stands in the corner; there we can rest upon roses and lavender, and throw salt in his eyes if he come near us."

"That will not do at all," said she; "besides, I know that the old mandarin was once betrothed to the pot-pourri vase, and no doubt there is still some slight friendship existing between them. No, there is no help for it, we must wander forth together into the wide world."

"Hast thou indeed the courage to go with me into the wide world?" asked the chimney-sweeper. "Hast thou considered how large it is, and that we may never return home again?"

"I have," replied she.

And the chimney-sweeper looked keenly at her, and then said, "My path leads through the chimney! hast thou indeed the courage to creep with me through the stove, through the flues and the tunnel? Well do I know the way! We shall mount up so high that they cannot come near us, and at the top there is a cavern that leads into the wide world."

And he led her to the door of the stove.

"Oh, how black it looks!" sighed she; however, she went on with him, through the flues and through the tunnel, where it was dark, pitch dark.

"Now we are in the chimney," said he; "and look, what a lovely star shines above us!"

And there was actually a star in the sky, shining right down upon them, as if to show them the way. And they crawled and crept—a fearful path was theirs—so high, so very high! but he guided and supported her, and showed her the best places whereon to plant her tiny porcelain feet, till they reached the edge of the chimney, where they sat down to rest, for they were very tired, and indeed not without reason.

Heaven with all its stars was above them, and the town with all its roofs lay beneath them; the wide, wide world surrounded them. The poor shepherdess had never imagined all this; she leant her little head on her chimney-sweeper's arm, and wept so vehemently that the gilding broke off from her waistband.

"This is too much!" exclaimed she. "This can I not endure! The world is all too large! Oh that I were once more upon the little table under the pier-glass! I shall never be happy till I am there again. I have followed thee out into the wide world, surely thou canst follow me home again, if thou lovest me!"

And the chimney-sweeper talked very sensibly to her, remind-ing her of the old Chinese mandarin and "the crooked-legged

Field-marshal-Major-General-Corporal-Sergeant," but she wept so bitterly, and kissed her little chimney-sweep so fondly, that at last he could not but yield to her request, unreasonable as it was.

So with great difficulty they crawled down the chimney, crept through the flues and the tunnel, and at length found themselves once more in the dark stove; but they still lurked behind the door, listening, before they would venture to return into the room. Everything was quite still; they peeped out: alas! on the ground lay the old Chinese mandarin. In attempting to follow the runaways, he had fallen down off the table and had broken into three pieces; his head lay shaking in a corner; "the crooked-legged Field-marshal-Major-General-Corporal-Sergeant" stood where he had always stood, thinking over what had happened.

"Oh, how shocking!" exclaimed the little shepherdess; "old grandfather is broken in pieces, and we are the cause! I shall never survive it!" and she wrung her delicate hands.

"He can be put together again," replied the chimney-sweeper. "He can very easily be put together; only be not so impatient! If they glue his back together, and put a strong rivet in his neck, then he will be as good as new again, and will be able to say plenty of unpleasant things to us."

"Do you really think so?" asked she. And then they climbed up the table to the place where they had stood before.

"See how far we have been!" observed the chimney-sweeper, "we might have spared ourselves all the trouble."

"If we could but have old grandfather put together!" said the shepherdess. "Will it cost very much?"

And he was put together; the family had his back glued and his neck riveted; he was as good as new, but could no longer nod his head.

"You have certainly grown very proud since you broke in pieces!" remarked the crooked-legged Field-marshal-Major-General-Corporal-Sergeant, "but I must say, for my part, I do not see that there is anything to be proud of. Am I to have her or am I not? Just answer me that!"

And the chimney-sweeper and the little shepherdess looked imploringly at the old mandarin; they were so afraid lest he should nod his head. But nod he could not, and it was disagreeable to him to tell a stranger that he had a rivet in his neck: so the young porcelain people always remained together; they blessed the grandfather's rivet, and loved each other till they broke in pieces.

The poor duckling was scorned by all

THE UGLY DUCKLING

IT WAS BEAUTIFUL IN THE COUNTRY, IT WAS SUMMER-TIME; the wheat was yellow, the oats were green, the hay was stacked up in the green meadows, and the stork paraded about on his long red legs, discoursing in Egyptian, which language he had learned from his mother. The fields and meadows were skirted by thick woods, and a deep lake lay in the midst of the woods.—Yes, it was indeed beautiful in the country! The sunshine fell warmly on an old mansion, surrounded by deep canals, and from the walls down to the water's edge there grew large burdock-leaves, so high that children could stand upright among them without being perceived. This place was as wild and unfrequented as the thickest part of the wood, and on that account a duck had chosen to make her nest there. She was sitting on her eggs; but the pleasure she had felt at first was now almost gone, because she had been there so long, and had so few visitors, for the other ducks preferred swimming on the canals to sitting among the burdock-leaves gossiping with her.

At last the eggs cracked one after another, "Tchick tchick!" All the eggs were alive, and one little head after another appeared. "Quack, quack," said the duck, and all got up as well as they could; they peeped about from under the green leaves, and as green is good for the eyes, their mother let them look as long as they pleased.

"How large the world is!" said the little ones, for they found their present situation very different to their former confined one, while yet in the egg-shells.

"Do you imagine this to be the whole of the world?" said the mother; "it extends far beyond the other side of the garden, to the pastor's field; but I have never been there. Are you all here?" And then she got up. "No, I have not got you all, the largest egg is still here. How long will this last? I am so weary of it!" And then she sat down again.

"Well, and how are you getting on?" asked an old duck, who had come to pay her a visit.

"This one egg keeps me so long," said the mother, "it will not break. But you should see the others; they are the prettiest little ducklings I have seen in all my days; they are all like their father,— the good-for-nothing fellow! he has not been to visit me once."

"Let me see the egg that will not break," said the old duck; "depend upon it, it is a turkey's egg. I was cheated in the same way once myself, and I had such trouble with the young ones; for they were afraid of the water, and I could not get them there. I called and scolded, but it was all of no use. But let me see the egg—ah yes! to be sure, that is a turkey's egg. Leave it, and teach the other little ones to swim."

"I will sit on it a little longer," said the duck. "I have been sitting so long, that I may as well spend the harvest here."

"It is no business of mine," said the old duck, and away she waddled.

The great egg burst at last, "Tchick, tchick," said the little one, and out it tumbled—but oh, how large and ugly it was! The duck looked at it, "That is a great, strong creature," said she, "none of the others are at all like it; can it be a young turkey-cock? Well, we shall soon find out, it must go into the water, though I push it in myself!"

The next day there was delightful weather, and the sun shone warmly upon all the green leaves when mother-duck with all her family went down to the canal; plump she went into the water, "Quack, quack," cried she, and one duckling after another jumped in. The water closed over their heads, but all came up again, and swam together in the pleasantest manner; their legs moved without effort. All were there, even the ugly grey one.

"No! it is not a turkey," said the old duck; "only see how prettily it moves its legs, how upright it holds itself; it is my own child! it is also really very pretty when one looks more closely at it; quack, quack, now come with me, I will take you into the world, introduce you in the duck-yard; but keep close to me, or some one may tread on you, and beware of the cat."

So they came into the duck-yard. There was a horrid noise; two families were quarrelling about the remains of an eel, which in the end was secured by the cat.

"See, my children, such is the way of the world," said the mother-duck, wiping her beak, for she too was fond of roasted eels. "Now use your legs," said she, "keep together, and bow to the old duck you see yonder. She is the most distinguished of all the fowls present, and is of Spanish blood, which accounts for her dignified appearance and manners. And look, she has a red rag on her leg; that is considered extremely handsome, and is the greatest distinction a duck can have. Don't turn your feet inwards; a well-educated duckling always keeps his legs far apart, like his father and mother, just so—look, now bow your necks, and say 'quack.'"

And they did as they were told. But the other ducks who were in the yard looked at them and said aloud, "Only see, now we have another brood, as if there were not enough of us already. And fie! how ugly that one is! We will not endure it"; and immediately one of the ducks flew at him, and bit him in the neck.

"Leave him alone," said the mother, "he is doing no one any harm."

"Yes, but he is so large, and so strange-looking, and there fore he shall be teased."

"Those are fine children that our good mother has," said the old duck with the red rag on her leg. "All are pretty except one, and that has not turned out well; I almost wish it could be hatched over again."

"That cannot be, please your highness," said the mother. "Certainly he is not handsome, but he is a very good child, and swims as well as the others, indeed rather better. I think he will grow like the others all in good time, and perhaps will look smaller. He stayed so long in the egg-shell, that is the cause of the difference," and she scratched the duckling's neck, and stroked his whole body. "Besides," added she, "he is a drake; I think he will be very strong, therefore it does not matter so much; he will fight his way through."

"The other ducks are very pretty," said the old duck, "pray make yourselves at home, and if you find an eel's head you can bring it to me."

And accordingly they made themselves at home.

But the poor little duckling, who had come last out of its egg-shell, and who was so ugly, was bitten, pecked, and teased by both ducks and hens. "It is so large," said they all. And the turkey-cock, who had come into the world with spurs on, and therefore fancied he was an emperor, puffed himself up like a ship in full sail, and marched up to the duckling quite red with passion. The poor little thing scarcely knew what to do; he was quite distressed, because he was so ugly, and because he was the jest of the poultry-yard.

So passed the first day, and afterwards matters grew worse and worse; the poor duckling was scorned by all. Even his brothers and sisters behaved unkindly, and were constantly saying, "The cat fetch thee, thou nasty creature!" The mother said, "Ah, if thou wert only far away!" The ducks bit him, the hens pecked him, and the girl who fed the poultry kicked him. He ran over the hedge; the little birds in the bushes were terrified. "That is because I am so ugly," thought the duckling, shutting his eyes, but he ran on. At last he came to a wide moor, where lived some wild ducks; here he lay the whole night, so tired and so comfortless. In the morning the wild ducks flew up, and perceived their new companion. "Pray, who are you?" asked they; and our little duckling turned himself in all directions, and greeted them as politely as possible.

"You are really uncommonly ugly," said the wild ducks; "however that does not matter to us, provided you do not marry into our families." Poor thing! he had never thought of marrying; he only begged permission to lie among the reeds, and drink the water of the moor.

He came to a wide moor

There he lay for two whole days—on the third day there came two wild geese, or rather ganders, who had not been long out of their egg-shells, which accounts for their impertinence.

"Hark ye," said they, "you are so ugly that we like you infinitely well; will you come with us, and be a bird of passage? On another moor, not far from this, are some dear, sweet, wild geese, as lovely creatures as have ever said 'hiss, hiss.' You are truly in the way to make your fortune, ugly as you are."

Bang! a gun went off all at once, and both wild geese were stretched dead among the reeds; the water became red with blood;—bang! a gun went off again, whole flocks of wild geese flew up from among the reeds, and another report followed.

There was a grand hunting party: the hunters lay in ambush all around; some were even sitting in the trees, whose huge branches stretched far over the moor. The blue smoke rose through the thick trees like a mist, and was dispersed as it fell over the water; the hounds splashed about in the mud, the reeds and rushes bent in all directions. How frightened the poor little duck was! He turned his head, thinking to hide it under his wings, and in a moment a most formidable-looking dog stood close to him, his tongue hanging out of his mouth, his eyes sparkling fearfully. He opened wide his jaws at the sight of our duckling, showed him his sharp white teeth, and, splash, splash! he was gone, gone without hurting him.

"Well! let me be thankful," sighed he, "I am so ugly, that even the dog will not eat me."

And now he lay still, though the shooting continued among the reeds, shot following shot.

The noise did not cease till late in the day, and even then the poor little thing dared not stir; he waited several hours before he looked around him, and then hastened away from the moor as fast as he could. He ran over fields and meadows, though the wind was so high that he had some difficulty in proceeding.

Towards evening he reached a wretched little hut, so wretched that it knew not on which side to fall, and therefore remained standing. The wind blew violently, so that our poor little duckling was obliged to support himself on his tail, in order to stand against it; but it became worse and worse. He then remarked that the door had lost one of its hinges, and hung so much awry that he could creep through the crevice into the room, which he did.

In this room lived an old woman, with her tom-cat and her hen; and the cat, whom she called her little son, knew how to set up his back and purr; indeed he could even emit sparks when stroked the wrong way. The hen had very short legs, and was therefore called "Cuckoo Shortlegs"; she laid very good eggs, and the old woman loved her as her own child.

The next morning the new guest was perceived; the cat began to mew, and the hen to cackle.

"What is the matter?" asked the old woman, looking round; however, her eyes were not good, so she took the young duckling to be a fat duck who had lost her way. "This is a capital catch," said she, "I shall now have duck's eggs, if it be not a drake: we must try."

And so the duckling was put to the proof for three weeks, but no eggs made their appearance.

Now the cat was the master of the house, and the hen was the mistress, and they used always to say, "We and the World," for they imagined themselves to be not only the half of the world, but also by far the better half. The duckling thought it was possible to be of a different opinion, but that the hen would not allow.

"Can you lay eggs?" asked she.

"No."

"Well, then, hold your tongue."

And the cat said, "Can you set up your back? can you purr?"

"No."

"Well, then, you should have no opinion when reasonable persons are speaking."

So the duckling sat alone in a corner, and was in a very bad humor; however, he happened to think of the fresh air and bright

And the cat said, "Can you set up your back? can you purr?"

sunshine, and these thoughts gave him such a strong desire to swim again that he could not help telling it to the hen.

"What ails you?" said the hen. "You have nothing to do, and, therefore, brood over these fancies; either lay eggs, or purr, then you will forget them."

"But it is so delicious to swim," said the duckling, "so delicious when the waters close over your head, and you plunge to the bottom."

"Well, that is a queer sort of a pleasure," said the hen; "I think you must be crazy. Not to speak of myself, ask the cat—he is the most sensible animal I know—whether he would like to swim or to plunge to the bottom of the water. Ask our mistress, the old woman—there is no one in the world wiser than she—do you think she would take pleasure in swimming, and in the waters closing over her head?"

"You do not understand me," said the duckling.

"What, we do not understand you! so you think yourself wiser than the cat, and the old woman, not to speak of myself. Do not fancy any such thing, child, but be thankful for all the kindness that has been shown you. Are you not lodged in a warm room, and have you not the advantage of society from which you can learn something? But you are a simpleton, and it is wearisome to have anything to do with you. Believe me, I wish you well. I tell you unpleasant truths, but it is thus that real friendship is shown. Come, for once give yourself the trouble to learn to purr, or to lay eggs."

"I think I will go out into the wide world again," said the duckling.

"Well, go," answered the hen.

So the duckling went. He swam on the surface of the water, he plunged beneath, but all animals passed him by, on account of his ugliness. And the autumn came, the leaves turned yellow and brown, the wind caught them and danced them about, the air was very cold, the clouds were heavy with hail or snow, and the raven sat on the hedge and croaked:—the poor duckling was certainly not very comfortable!

One evening, just as the sun was setting with unusual brilliancy, a flock of large beautiful birds rose from out of the brushwood; the duckling had never seen anything so beautiful before; their plumage was of a dazzling white, and they had long, slender necks. They were swans; they uttered a singular cry, spread out their long, splendid wings, and flew away from these cold regions to warmer countries, across the open sea. They flew so high, so very high! and the little ugly duckling's feelings were so strange; he turned round and round in the water like a mill-wheel, strained his neck to look after them, and sent forth such a loud and strange cry, that it almost frightened himself.—Ah! he could not forget them, those noble birds! those happy birds! When he could see them no longer, he plunged to the bottom of the water, and when he rose again was almost beside himself. The duckling knew not what the birds were called, knew not whither they were flying, yet he loved them as he had never before loved anything; he envied them not, it would never have occurred to him to wish such beauty for himself; he would have been quite contented if the duck in the duck-yard had but endured his company—the poor ugly animal!

And the winter was so cold, so cold! The duckling was obliged to swim round and round in the water, to keep it from freezing;

but every night the opening in which he swam became smaller and smaller; it froze so that the crust of ice crackled; the duckling was obliged to make good use of his legs to prevent the water from freezing entirely; at last, wearied out, he lay stiff and cold in the ice.

Early in the morning there passed by a peasant, who saw him, broke the ice in pieces with his wooden shoe, and brought him home to his wife.

He now revived; the children would have played with him, but our duckling thought they wished to tease him, and in his terror jumped into the milk-pail, so that the milk was spilled about the room: the good woman screamed and clapped her hands; he flew thence into the pan where the butter was kept, and thence into the meal-barrel, and out again, and then how strange he looked!

The woman screamed, and struck at him with the tongs; the children ran races with each other trying to catch him, and laughed and screamed likewise. It was well for him that the door stood open; he jumped out among the bushes into the new-fallen snow—he lay there as in a dream.

But it would be too melancholy to relate all the trouble and misery that he was obliged to suffer during the severity of the winter—he was lying on a moor among the reeds, when the sun began to shine warmly again, the larks sang, and beautiful spring had returned.

And once more he shook his wings. They were stronger than formerly, and bore him forwards quickly, and before he was well aware of it, he was in a large garden where the apple trees stood in full bloom, where the syringas sent forth their fragrance and hung their long green branches down into the winding canal.

Oh, everything was so lovely, so full of the freshness of spring! And out of the thicket came three beautiful white swans. They displayed their feathers so proudly, and swam so lightly, so lightly! The duckling knew the glorious creatures, and was seized with a strange melancholy.

"I will fly to them, those kingly birds!" said he. "They will kill me, because I, ugly as I am, have presumed to approach them; but it matters not, better to be killed by them than to be bitten by the ducks, pecked by the hens, kicked by the girl who feeds the poultry, and to have so much to suffer during the winter!" He flew into the water, and swam towards the beautiful creatures—they saw him and shot forward to meet him. "Only kill me," said the poor animal, and he bowed his head low, expecting death,—but what did he see in the water?—he saw beneath him his own form, no longer that of a plump, ugly, grey bird—it was that of a swan.

It matters not to have been born in a duck-yard, if one has been hatched from a swan's egg.

The good creature felt himself really elevated by all the troubles and adversities he had experienced. He could now rightly estimate his own happiness, and the larger swans swam round him, and stroked him with their beaks.

Some little children were running about in the garden; they threw grain and bread into the water, and the youngest exclaimed, "There is a new one!"—the others also cried out, "Yes, there is a new swan come!" and they clapped their hands, and danced around. They ran to their father and mother, bread and cake were thrown into the water, and every one said, "The new one is the best, so young, and so beautiful!" and the old swans bowed before him. The young swan felt quite ashamed, and hid his head under

And every one said, "The new one is the best"

his wings; he scarcely knew what to do, he was all too happy, but still not proud, for a good heart is never proud.

He remembered how he had been persecuted and derided, and he now heard every one say he was the most beautiful of all beautiful birds. The syringas bent down their branches towards him low into the water, and the sun shone so warmly and brightly—he shook his feathers, stretched his slender neck, and in the joy of his heart said, "How little did I dream of so much happiness when I was the ugly, despised duckling!"

Beware of him, dear child

THE NAUGHTY BOY

HERE WAS ONCE AN OLD POET, SUCH A GOOD, HONEST OLD poet! He was sitting alone in his own little room on a very stormy evening; the wind was roaring with out, and the rain poured down in torrents. But the old man sat cozily by his warm stove, the fire was blazing brightly, and some apples were roasting in front of it.

"Those poor people who have no roof to shelter them to-night will, most assuredly, not have a dry thread left on their skin," said the kind-hearted old man.

"Oh, open the door! open the door! I am so cold, and quite wet through besides—open the door!" cried a voice from without. The voice was like a child's, and seemed half-choked with sobs. "Rap, rap, rap!" it went on knocking at the door, whilst the rain still kept streaming down from the clouds, and the wind rattled among the window-panes.

"Poor thing!" said the old poet; and he arose and opened the door. There stood a little boy, almost naked; the water trickled down from his long flaxen hair; he was shivering with cold, and had he been left much longer out in the street, he must certainly have perished in the storm.

"Poor boy!" said the old poet again, taking him by the hand, and leading him into his room. "Come to me, and we'll soon make thee warm again, and I will give thee some wine, and some roasted apples for thy supper, my pretty child!"

And, of a truth, the boy was exceedingly pretty. His eyes shone as bright as stars, and his hair, although dripping with water, curled in beautiful ringlets. He looked quite like a little cherub, but he was very pale, and trembled in every limb with cold. In his hand he held a pretty little cross-bow, but it seemed entirely spoilt by the rain, and the colors painted on the arrows all ran one into another.

The old poet sat down again beside the stove, and took the little boy in his lap; he wrung the water out of his streaming hair, warmed the child's hands within his own, and gave him mulled wine to drink. The boy soon became himself again, the rosy color returned to his cheeks, he jumped down from the old man's lap, and danced around him on the floor.

"Thou art a merry fellow!" said the poet. "Thou must tell me thy name."

"They call me Cupid," replied the boy. "Don't you know me? There lies my bow; ah, you can't think how capitally I can shoot! See, the weather is fine again now; the moon is shining bright."

"But thy bow is spoilt," said the old man.

"That would be a sad disaster, indeed," remarked the boy, as he took the bow in his hand and examined it closely. "Oh, it is quite dry by this time, and it is not a bit damaged; the string, too, is quite strong enough, I think. However, I may as well try it!" He then drew his bow, placed an arrow before the string, took his aim, and shot direct into the old poet's heart. "Now you may

PLATE 16.
He jumped down from the old man's lap and
danced around him on the floor

be sure that my cross-bow is not spoilt!" cried he, as, with a loud laugh, he ran away.

The naughty boy! This was, indeed, ungrateful of him, to shoot to the heart the good old man who had so kindly taken him in, warmed him, and dried his clothes, given him sweet wine, and nice roasted apples for supper!

The poor poet lay groaning on the ground, for the arrow had wounded him sorely. "Fie, for shame, Cupid!" cried he, "thou art a wicked boy! I will tell all good children how thou hast treated me, and bid them take heed and never play with thee, for thou wilt assuredly do them a mischief, as thou hast done to me."

All the good boys and girls to whom he related this story were on their guard against the wicked boy, Cupid; but, notwithstanding, he made fools of them again and again, he is so terribly cunning! When the students are returning home from lecture, he walks by their side, dressed in a black gown, and with a book under his arm. They take him to be a fellow-student, and so they suffer him to walk arm-in-arm with them, just as if he were one of their intimate friends. But whilst they are thus familiar with him, all of a sudden he thrusts his arrows into their bosoms. Even when young girls are going to church, he will follow and watch for his opportunity: he is always waylaying people. In the theatre, he sits in the great chandelier, and kindles such a bright, hot flame, men fancy it a lamp, but they are soon undeceived. He wanders about in the royal gardens and all the public walks, making mischief everywhere; nay, once he even shot thy father and mother to the heart! Only ask them, dear child, and they will certainly tell thee all about it. In fine, this fellow, this Cupid, is a very wicked boy! Do not play with him! He waylays everybody, boys and girls, youths and maidens, men and women, rich and poor, old and young. Only think of this: he once shot an arrow into thy good old grandmother's heart! It happened a long time ago, and she has recovered from the wound, but she will never forget him, depend upon it.

Fie, for shame! wicked Cupid! Is he not a mischievous boy? Beware of him, beware of him, dear child!

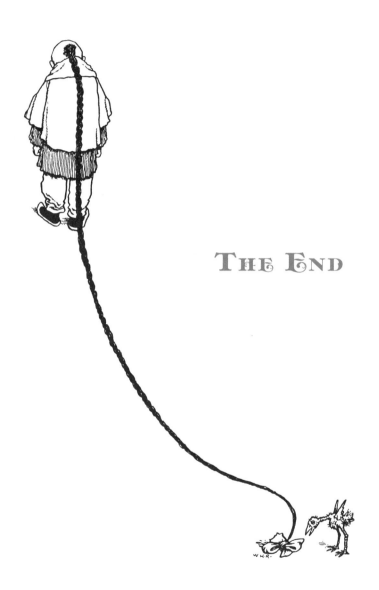

THE END